PENGUIN BOOKS

THE POWER ABOVE US ALL

Ronaldo Soledad Vivo Jr is a Filipino novelist, musician, and graphic artist. He is the author of the novels *Ang Kapangyarihang Higit sa Ating Lahat (The Power Above Us All)* and *Ang Bangin sa Ilalim ng Ating mga Paa (The Abyss Beneath Our Feet)*. He has been recognized for his contributions to Philippine literature as the finalist for the Madrigal Gonzalez Best First Book Award and the National Book Awards. He is a recipient of both the Gawad Bienvenido Lumbera and the Premyong LIRA. He is the founder of Ungaz Press, a collective of writers from the town of Pateros. He is also an award-winning filmmaker whose short films have been screened at festivals and cinemas in the Philippines and overseas. As a musician, he runs Sound Carpentry Recordings, which releases music on cassette, CD, and vinyl for worldwide distribution.

Karl R. de Mesa is a longreads journalist and photographer who has reported on stories in the Philippines, Hong Kong, Myanmar, and Singapore. He is an award-winning author of horror fiction and reportage books—finalists for the Philippine National Book Awards for journalism and non-fiction. His photo essays have appeared on *CNN Philippines Life* and *Likhaan: The Journal of Contemporary Philippine Literature*. Ronaldo Vivo Jr's *The Power Above Us All* is the first novel he has translated. More at https://linktr.ee/karlrdemesa

ADVANCE PRAISE FOR
THE POWER ABOVE US ALL

'I have just closed the book with fresh astonishment at the storytelling skill on display. Dodong and Butsok's narrative are smartly woven, and, in its weaving, the playfulness is apparent. Which makes the book exciting to read because it promises a new way to make and write novels.'

—Allan Derain, professor, writer

'The hairs on my body stood up each time I read a page of this novel. In the middle of the book, in fact, I sent a text to the writer asking if I had to ready myself and what level of mental preparedness I had to have to tackle the rest of the book. This novel will no doubt break you if you're fragile.'

—Norman Wilwayco, Filipino novelist

'There's a vulca-seal lyricism in Ronaldo Vivo Jr's prose—something that simultaneously blunts then sharpens every blow. Hurts to read yet I can't stop turning pages.'

—Angelo Suarez, Filipino poet, activist

The Power Above Us All

Ronaldo Soledad Vivo Jr

Translated by

Karl R. de Mesa

PENGUIN BOOKS

An imprint of Penguin Random House

PENGUIN BOOKS

Penguin Books is an imprint of the Penguin Random House group of companies whose addresses can be found at global.penguinrandomhouse.com

Published by Penguin Random House SEA Pte Ltd
40 Penjuru Lane, #03-12, Block 2
Singapore 609216

First published in Penguin Books by Penguin Random House SEA 2024

10 9 8 7 6 5 4 3 2 1

This is a work of fiction. Names, characters, places and incidents are either the product of the author's imagination or are used fictitiously, and any resemblance to any actual person, living or dead, events or locales is entirely coincidental.

The Power Above Us All includes elements that might not be suitable for some readers. Rape, physical and sexual violence, racial slurs, incest, child sexual abuse, and self harm are present in the story. Readers who may be sensitive to these elements please take note.

ISBN 9789815204711

Typeset in Garamond by MAP Systems, Bengaluru, India

www.penguin.sg

For Olivia Himig
Nihl, Gabriel, Isabelle and Alonzo Louis

Foreword

We must use analogies to declare something good, beautiful, or apt. This is the way a work in literature comes to be considered canon. Yet great works don't always follow the process of canonization and there were always works that objected, rebelled, or refused to obey. And thus are books of protest, transgression and, in the case of *The Power Above Us All* by Ronaldo Vivo Jr, made into the beginning of such works that were influenced by the *novela negra*. Things were added, changed, demolished. It is likely that this is how newness is born, through a contravention of the tradition we'd become accustomed to.

How to compare those works of inversions or opposition? There lies the difficulty. Like comparing our own universe to a dark universe. Like the search for both matter and antimatter within the confines of regular matter. Present yet unbeheld. Like looking at something at night with the lights out and knowing full well that being unseen does not automatically mean being unable to hold it in our mind's eye. And how shall we try to understand a work that's been deflected, concealed, even snubbed?

We may compare it to garbage. It is simply all around us. Something we cover, push away, throw out of sight and, as much as possible, would want collected in the early morning by trash men so that when we wake up it's already magically disappeared. We do not want foulness or filth. If people take on garbage-like qualities, what then? Shall they be thrown away and hidden? Covered and ostracized? The scenes in this book waft with an unpleasant reek from start to finish.

Yet we know full well a thing is not first made into garbage. Many times, it still has utility or value even when its time has come and gone. Similarly, people aren't born trash. While some rise and progress, as some become wealthy, there is always an underclass that will remain. These are the dregs of society. These are the lumpen, the anti-social, and those deemed sans worth to society. This is the novel's theme, nurtured and developed. People aren't born bad, see.

This book challenges us. Look into the darkest zone of the darkness. That's where it wants us to visit and peek, the place it wants us to understand. There are those who are condemned and we are indeed part of those, the doomed; who shall say otherwise? What grave mistakes did we commit? And where were we found lacking? We live in one universe and those invisible to us or those we refuse to behold are still part of that.

Thank you, Ronaldo Vivo Jr, for disturbing us. And in your disruption of our thoughts as this book knocks us on the skull, may we be educated, may those who read these words regain their senses.

—Jun Cruz Reyes
20th and 21st Madrigal Gonzales First Book Award
Citation for *The Power Above Us All*

I

The Power Above Us All

1

In this moment three things remain bright in my memory. Three things only: Che's smile, my final reminder to my friend Buldan, and the scent and taste of the soup of a disgusting toilet mixed with, hell, the taste of someone's hotdog-shaped shit—some pig cop from precinct nine.

Past midnight. Outside the San Joaquin 7-Eleven, Buldan and I were hanging steady. Smoking, watching. Across the street two uniformed pigs were walking to where we stood. We kept conversing calmly but we were nervous at their approach. Both police officers walked past us and straight into the 7-Eleven. We exhaled, relieved. Both of us also concurred that it was time to change locations

That was till we noticed the commotion inside. I told Buldan to see what was up. Just the two pigs arguing loudly with two teen boys, he said, and that the young men both looked way too smooth-skinned to be any good if a fight went down.

Well, I thought, *it's good timing these two teenage dirt bags showed up. We wouldn't need to move at all now.*

Seconds later, another young man exited the convenience store. He looked no older than nineteen to me, if a day. Quick tap on Buldan's shoulder. He returned my gesture with a nod.

Before we walked on, I handed him another stick of Fortune Lights. Buldan slotted the cigarette behind his right earlobe, then he pushed off in the same direction our third teen went. I remained at the 7-Eleven, continuing to surveil the two police officers inside.

When I finished my cigarette—still waiting for Buldan's text message—I stepped into the convenience store. Time to cool myself with the air-conditioning and also get closer to see what was what.

I sat on one of the dining area's chairs and eavesdropped on the exchange. Ah, the teens were being hassled for IDs. The stylishly bearded youths already had curly-haired legs despite their smooth appearance and yet they were still being asked for IDs for the beer they wanted to buy. Clever pigs. Whatever happened next, the two police would come away with some extra cash for their meth-buying money.

Not ten minutes in I got a text from Buldan saying to meet back at the room.

I knew Buldan was nervous. 'Meet halfway beyond,' said the text message. This meant he'd unfortunately wounded the kid.

The two teens were being escorted out by the two officers. Still quacking loudly at the harassment. When they were gone, I stepped out too.

I hailed a jeepney. This time of night, Che's place would be hot. I wanted to eyeball the situation first before going home to the room. Only a few of us were on this commute; a pregnant teen, two muscular guys holding hands, and a man so drunk his head was already between his legs, nose dipping low enough it almost touched his own vomit that had spread on the filthy floor.

In the doubly cold breath of the early morning, the answer to the chill—for those who could afford it—was heat for the skin and satisfaction for the loins. Likely the same reason why beerhouses are jumping during these hours. The ride was a yawn fest.

I really wanted to add something more to what I was going to hand over to Che. She'd run out of rice and milk for the two kids, she'd told me.

Her salary? She said it had already gone to pay the rent. Thing was, I had exactly enough in my pocket. Doubtful that I could score much of anything if I were to actually stick up this ride. Though I did want to.

Pregnant girl, for one. Might go into labour with the fear. Lose the baby. That would be on my conscience. People always think we don't have a fucking conscience but they should really look at the politicians and priests. I also hear the police around these parts are all young rookies. Makes it hard to screw up and all. See, if the pigs are new then they'll take turns getting baptized on account of my sorry ass. And I'd rather not end up on the wrong side of a piggy baptismal rite.

'Para! Getting off,' I called out to the driver and knocked on the jeepney's ceiling.

'Pulling over,' replied the jeepney driver tiredly.

I got off at the distance of a few KTV bars before Che's workplace. I did remember that, at this hour, Che's place was hot. The key in such a climate was indeed maintaining distance.

I hung out in front of Karuza Club, down the road were a funeral parlour and a hardware store. Then, after them was the Red Butterfly where Che worked. At Mang Rey's vendor stand I speared a few fishballs while waiting.

'Elmer here?' I asked Mang Rey.

'Y-yeah, he just c-came in a few minutes ago,' said Mang Rey almost in a whisper. The uncanny effect of how bastards made sure they were at the top of the food chain was almost admirable. Even saying their name made people weak in the knees.

'And Mayet, she out here?' I added.

'Not yet,' replied Mang Rey.

Nodding, I continued spearing fishballs with my wooden stick. Between chewing and swallowing, I heard Elmer's voice.

He had just come out. Even from afar, I could sense the whirlwind the sonuvabitch brought with him. Elmer's arm grasped Che tight around her waist. Mayet followed, hailing a taxi for the two. Che went in first, the bastard followed.

When the taxi was almost out of sight, Mayet turned to me and waved. I sprinted to her.

'You haven't paid,' Mang Rey called after me.

'I'll come back!' I shouted over my shoulder.

I pushed forward to Mayet.

'Dodong, you hard-headed idiot,' she opened.

'I kept my distance, 'Yet!' I reasoned.

'Tsk! Hmmm, what now?'

'Well, how's your friend?'

'You know well enough she'll be riding Elmer's saddle for a while,' she shook her head.

'I got Che's rice and milk money.' From the back pocket of my jeans I grabbed the cash and handed it over. Mayet put the wad of cash into her bra.

'It'll be morning by the time I can hand it to her. Same time she'll be back, most likely.'

'Motherfucking Elmer,' I spat.

She slapped my shoulder. 'Watch what you say, Dodong. Someone hears you out here we'll both be getting it,' Mayet said, her tone sharp. I handed her a cigarette. I fired it up when she put it in her mouth. Then, I lit my own.

'Must be heavenly being a filthy pig,' I continued. 'Free beer, free pussy.' Mayet sighed and shook her head at my stubborn ways.

2

After getting her brains fried with the blessing of melted meth, smoked in a *palara*, a makeshift foil pipe made out of Reynolds Wrap, she started serving the man who was considered the saviour of the club where she danced. He also owned the *gak* she'd just smoked.

She dove between those big, filthy thighs. Started tonguing his hairy balls while massaging the small cock. An act she'd never be able to accomplish without the help of hard drugs. Every crack, crevice, and corner got a dose of her saliva. Later, her mouth replaced her hand, lips small and flushed red.

The man's moan resonated through the room.

After worshipping the beast's small cock, she laid back on the bed, limbs akimbo, legs spread, revealing a small yet engorged vagina. The beast lowered himself to that delicate flower. He poked her clit using his yellowish tongue. Despite valiantly resisting, there were times her hips and thighs spasmed from the pleasure. She did not look down on him. Not a peek. Her eyes had been shut from the start of his ministrations.

The odious beast came up for air and grasped his cock. Ever so slowly he inserted it into her wetness. Started driving, pumping into a groove, really giving it to her hard. His moans echoed across the room's corners. And she heard nothing.

The beast licked her neck, up to her cheeks and face. She closed her lips, avoiding his kiss. He noticed this. Stopped, pulled out of her, and went to the side table. Pistol came out of its holster. He pointed it at her groin, and grabbed her face, which had zero emotion on it.

'Sonuvabitch, you whore. Whatcha looking for?' Eyes sparking hellfire.

Only silence from her. Something that served to goad the beast.

'You disrespecting me?' He released the magazine.

Pushing the bullets off, all of them came out of the mag and pinged to the floor. That done, he forcibly opened her legs, driving the cold magazine into her pussy.

'AAAAAAHWWW!' Resistance shattered. She couldn't help but writhe from the pain. When he pulled the mag out a trickle of oily blood followed. Red stains covered the white bed sheet.

'Ah, dumb bitch, go wash up!' He said, throwing her the towel.

As the blood flowed down her legs, so did her tears.

Walking to the bathroom, the beast of a man was already folding up a new palara. The use of the Reynolds Wrap had already lifted him up from the common ruck of *shabu* smokers, who could only afford cigarette box foil.

'I better not find out that whoreson Dodong still sniffing after you, Che, or they'll find you both under old newspapers! Do not test me on this,' he warned, then inhaled the white smoke from the palara pipe. In the bathroom, reddish water bathed the tiles. She could only stare at the bubbling mix of soap, water, and blood.

'What's taking you so long, stupid bitch?' Shouted the beast.

She opened the shower, closed her eyes and tilted her chin up to the water, cleansing herself, repulsed by it all. He kicked down the comfort room door. She tried not to flinch at the invasion, the ruckus. Carried on bathing. Eyes closed. He grabbed her, greasy hands on her neck and arm, dragged her to the sink, aiming to penetrate her from behind so that, when she lifted her head up to the mirror, she would be able to get a full view of his maniacal face. He too was watching her in turn.

She couldn't help but open her eyes. What she saw in the mirror above that sink was a living nightmare. She shut her eyes again.

3

You'll know it when you're near Dreamland. Fragrant. Like soap. Nearby where Buldan and I call home is a detergent factory, smack right on the borders of our place within the Inners—the Looban. This means no matter how much the brutish citizens of the Dreamland live like fiends, they still know the difference between stinky and ambrosial. This has imbued the residents with a certain snobbishness whenever they step out. Meaning, because of all the laundry soap smell in the air, their noses have been sensitized against the rancid or rotten—the default scent of the city. Unlike its borders though, the navel of the Dreamland smells like a fetid, cursed place. This also means you can easily tell when you reach the centre of our blessed inner-city community.

Buldan was smoking gak when I came in. The moron didn't know how to close the damn door. Then again, with how our door looked you couldn't really hide anything anyway. The thing was a piece of rusted aluminium roofing with holes, barely held together by mouldy, repurposed tarps. What was the value in hiding, anyway? Everyone in the Dreamland was a meth head and a dope fiend.

'Going solo today, ah,' I greeted Buldan.

'Just leftovers,' he replied.

'Ahhh . . .' I stalled as a retort.

'Where ya been, then?' He asked.

'Ahhh . . . dropped by Anton's place, might have a gig. Never know.'

'Bullshiiit. When ya introducing me to your chick?'

'Chick? Shut up, whoreson. Told you I came from Anton's, bastard.'

'Alright, alright. Let's say Grandma believes ya.'

I changed the subject. 'How much did we score from the kid anyway?'

'Three *thou*, Dong,' he said, then gulped in a toke.

'Closed at three?' I wanted to be sure.

'Closed.'

'Where did you hurt the kid?'

'Neck. Just a surface cut—the little bastard kept wriggling.'

'Nervous hands, more like.'

'Fuck that.'

'Cell phone?' I asked.

'iTouch. Cabinet, under my hat,' Buldan said.

I stepped to the cabinet and got the iTouch. Turned it over in my hand.

'One five would move this quick?'

'Make it two thou, they'll haggle it down for sure.'

'Sounds good.'

I got on the mattress and leaned on the wall. Also happens to be the wall of our neighbour Helen, who was a pimp. So focused was Buldan on the foil pipe that he even inhaled the smoke from our Katol mosquito repellent.

'Dong, want some?' He offered.

I crawled to Buldan and got the foil and tooter. While I smoked up, Buldan kept scratching his leg. *The bastard has started tripping*, I thought.

'Everyone knows you're a lazy twat, but get your shit together to bathe, at least. No wonder people think we're addicts,' I berated him.

Buldan intensified his scratching. I noticed the leg was bleeding. I let go of the foil pipe.

'Stop that, hoy!' I swatted his hand away from the bleeding leg. The wound was fresh and was definitely not just from his nails. 'Hell happened there?'

'Was at Botong's earlier.'

'Then it wasn't just three thousand from the kid?'

'Only brought out two hundred. Botong said he was taxing me the rest. I swear he'd put a pig with twelve side chicks to shame!'

'Then? What did he do?'

'Shouldered me against Aling Supreng's wall and smashed a Redhorse on my foot.'

'Didn't fight?'

'Fighting Botong would be pointless, and I tell ya, the bastard doesn't scrap fair.'

'That whoreson, he should find his own way to fund his vices.' I picked up the tooter, foil pipe, and lighter. Went back to sucking meth smoke.

'Good thing Marco was there to pull Botong off.'

'Don't believe those shitheads, they're all in it with Botong. Idiots got no way to score so they hassle other people trying to score.'

'Shit. Well, let's just let it go, Dong,' he urged.

'Let me have two hundred from that three.'

'What for?' Buldan asked.

'Gin.'

Buldan grabbed two hundred-peso bills and handed them to me. 'Buy some Happy Reds. And half Fortune Lights.'

I hurried outside. Only Aling Supreng's sari-sari store was open at this hour. And if I happened to encounter Botong and his gang, then so be it. *Bahala na.* Didn't have nothing else but two hundred on me. Quiet tonight in the hood. No brawls, nobody yawping at nothing. No knifings, no rioting boys who'd had too much of Mang Max's spring rolls. Quiet's pretty strange, that. At Aling Supreng's there was a table with small pails and Redhorse bottles laid out. Nobody around, though. I used a 5 peso coin to knock on the store wall.

'Anyone hoooome?' I called.

Aling Supreng came out. 'Buying, Dong?'

'Two gin rounders. And a Tang Orange.'

While she was getting our round bottles, I kept checking behind me.

'*Ate*, elder sister, the guys who were drinking here around?'

'I heard the pests were heading to Felix's.'

'Ahhh . . . that's where they'll continue their drinking party.'

'To score, more like. Nobody goes to Felix unless you're buying meth.'

'Ah, true. Those whoresons are all addicts,' I added. Putting down the hundred, I grabbed the plastic with the gin and the Tang.

'Just remembered, Ate. Let me get the whole line of Reds.'

She turned on her heel from counting change in front of me and pulled out the Happy Reds on the shelf.

'Dong, open that plastic,' she said.

I held the translucent bag open, and she threw the cigarettes in like a basketball. Great shot. Aling Supreng went back to counting my change, but as she did, I could hear a posse of voices, the harmonic brag and swagger getting louder as they approached. Laughing. Definitely a group. Very likely Botong and his gang.

'Ate, I'll come back for that change, ha,' I told Aling Supreng.

'Ha? Well, alright.'

I dashed away and headed for the room.

No looking back.

* * *

Buldan was still scratching his leg when I came back. This time with a comb.

'Hoy, you whoreson, stop that,' I berated him.

'Itches, man!' He reasoned.

'Nope, you're just tripping!'

Bastard still kept at it. I sat beside him and pulled out the gin round bottles, opened one with my teeth.

'I said desist in thy scraping, you bastard,' and swatted his hand away. I poured gin on the fresh wound.

'Oh fuck, Dong, don't waste that!' Buldan said, panicked.

From my brief I pulled out my lighter and quickly ignited the alcohol on the wound.

Buldan freaked. 'Fucking whoreson, cunty bastard, that burns! Burns!'

I held both his arms down so he couldn't reach the burning leg. He was too strong for me though. Likely from all the hard drugs in his system. Buldan got free and grabbed the pillow, putting out the fire.

'Your mother's a whore, Dong! You're the one tripping, crazy bastard,' Buldan said, irritated

'Still itchy? Still hurts?'

Looking at his wound he saw that it had now partially dried. I estimated that the idiot had also come down from his high. At least a bit. Maybe a lot. Burning leg can do that. Leaning on the wall, he shook his head.

'Mix that shit up,' he sighed.

'Fine.'

'Fortune?'

'Fuck, I forgot!'

'Look in my jeans. Should be some still in there.'

'Great.'

Out of the room I walked out gingerly with a jug, the Tang, and the remaining gin bottle. Fetched water from Lani's faucet—open twenty-four hours for freeloading neighbours like Buldan and I. I filled the jug less than halfway. Mixed in the Tang. Gin went in and only then did I taste the blend. *Fucking delicious! Just the right proportions, fuck yeah.*

Then, I remembered. Because I was rushing so much to get away from the store and Botong, I had forgotten the ice. Sonuvabitch.

4

'You lovebirds done?' Mayet greeted him when he came out the room. A sweaty Dong could only nod and a smile. Mayet went in past him. Che was lying on her belly. Lids closed but awake.

'Girl, he say anything about your bruises?' Mayet asked Che.

'Of course he was angry. Cried about it.'

'Crying huh, really now. Dong's such a drama queen,' Mayet chided.

'Said he felt helpless.'

'Yeeeeah . . . Does he even stand a chance against Elmer?'

'With me he does . . . I love Dodong.'

'Sure. But Elmer owns you.'

Silence filled the room. Che was scrambling for something to say. Mayet seemed shocked at her own outburst.

'I want to thank you, 'Yet,' Che finally said.

'What for?' Asked Mayet.

'Your place is the only way we can meet, so I really want to thank you again for that.'

'It's nothing,' Mayet stroked Che's hair.

Dodong was watching Che from outside the room. He couldn't help but still see the bruises despite the blanket covering most of her body. It was to him a fresh experience of hell that resisted forgetting. When he tried to inhale back his snot the tears fell down. He could do nothing for Che. He could do nothing against the fear and cowardice that he felt about Elmer. 'Inutile dickless twat', were the words singing in his head. Wiping his tears, he then stepped into the room.

'Che, 'Yet? I'm buying our dinner,' he said, interrupting their conversation.

'Get me siomai, Dong,' said Che.

'Oh no, girl, the siomai dumpling house on the outside has moved, changed their location to J.P. Rizal,' said Mayet.

'Ah, okay let's go for barbeque,' Che shrugged.

'Yeah, I want isaw and ears,' Mayet chirped.

'Che, what about you?' Dodong asked.

'Up to you, Dong.'

'Alright, isaw chicken intestines and pig ears for Mayet. And I'll think of something for you, Che.'

Dodong walked towards the nearest barbeque near the outside, which was Mang Max's. People were clustered around his grillery, waiting for their orders. But because Dodong and Mang Max were buddies, his orders always got express processing.

'Annie, where's Mang Max?' Dodong asked the cook manning the grill.

'And what's your order, Dong?' She asked, her tone sharp.

Dodong chuckled. 'Ten isaw, four ears, three pork barbecues.'

'Dong, your style sucks! Pretending to look for my uncle Tiyo Max, but all you really want is to jump the line.'

'C'mon, let's have peace! I'll find you a nice American boyfriend. Plenty of them where I work,' Dodong said cheerfully then laughed again.

'No joke?' Annie's face lit up.

'Oh yeah, somebody that's the spitting image of Tom Cruise'

'Ayyy. That's no good, Dong.'

'What, why?'

'I like . . . Black guys,' she whispered shyly.

'Ahhh? Okay. Annie, you're a naughty one, ha!' Dodong laughed hard.

Annie laughed with him. 'Joker. I'll get to cooking your order now, don't worry.'

'Thanks Annie! I'll search the place for a seven-footer Black dude!'

'Clown!' Annie said, laughing.

Dodong closely scoped out the people as he waited for his order. He was desperate for money and had no idea what to do with the increasingly thickening crowd. He wasn't a pickpocket. See, there's a big difference between a robber and a pickpocket. Robbing people was considered manlier and had a more humane process to it, because when you held people up at gunpoint you let them know they now had to say goodbye to their beloved coin and possessions. The pickpocket meanwhile left his victims a paranoid wreck.

His order came after almost fifteen minutes of boredom. Fast enough, considering other customers had lined up before him. Mang Max's curbside barbecue operation was always popular, despite the fact that in the mornings it only sold lumpiang toge, the spring rolls made of mung bean sprouts were the favourite snack of the residents in the Inners.

With a plastic bag full of the grilled food in his hands, Dodong started the walk back to Mayet's. The alleys that were near empty when he passed by not twenty minutes ago were now thronged with people—folks who looked like rubberneckers and gossips you found at any calamity. Dodong squeezed his way through the thick crowd that to him smelled like armpits. From beyond the crowd, he could hear the unmistakable ruckus of a beating. Such sounds were coming from Mayet's place. His gut warned him something bad was happening and his heart skipped a beat from the anxiety. Nearing the edge of the throng, Dodong whispered to a shaven-headed man, tattoos covering both arms, who stood on a small stool so he could better see the action.

'Boss, what do we got here?' Dodong asked, looking up at the skinhead tattoo guy with his head above the crowd.

'Plainclothes police apparently, these guys. I think Mayet's friend owes them and they've come to collect.'

Dodong felt a sudden chill spread through his nape and back. The sounds of cursing and crying plus the damned clattering of furniture and bodies grew louder in his ears. The skinhead's spit had fallen on his face. He wiped it away with his shirt. Dodong turned back and walked away—still in his grip were the grilled meats they were supposed to eat for dinner.

5

We scored a matron yesterday. Old woman was dressed like a teenager. She was Buldan's friend's contact. Craved the cock. I let her taste it then destroyed her with it. Her wallet had seven thou. Pair of gold earrings, three rings also made of gold, and a silver necklace with a heart pendant. Told Buldan I wanted the necklace when we split the loot. He shrugged and agreed.

Che would get that necklace. Sometimes I had it in me to make her blush. Even a bit, at least. I asked Buldan for a silver cleaner since he was going downtown anyway. Something to make the thing look shiny and smell new.

I went to Puregold while waiting for Buldan, buying groceries for Che and her kids. Diapers, milk, canned goods, noodles. Managed to fill up two plastic bags. At the counter, I asked the cashier to maybe put it all in a box so Buldan wouldn't be able to easily peek into what I'd bought. I'd tell him they're old clothes to be given away.

Merienda with siomai before I left the grocery store and I remembered Che as I ate. Early days we were good just eating siomai, you know. As long as we were together. Truth be told, we haven't really gone out on a date, even at a breakfast place for tapsilog. How could we, when the whole fucking town was one huge CCTV and wherever we thought we could go was off-limits because, as Che rightly claimed, Elmer had eyes everywhere and was connected to damn well everyone? Became my habit to buy siomai for a viand whenever we would rendezvous at Mayet's.

Devoured two more siomai orders then ordered one more for Buldan. Just so I could say I brought something home for him.

Outside Puregold I waited for a tricycle I could hitch on. From a distance I spotted our friend Jeffrey riding on one, a motorcycle with a covered passenger cab on the right side.

'Jepoy!' I called to him waving, even though he was still a ways off. He waved back and stepped on the gas.

'Where you headed, Dong?' He asked.

'Hopefully home! You?'

'Headed there too but only until Butsok's place.'

'Great. Let me ride with you. I'll be able to walk home from Butsok's the rest of the way.'

I loaded up the box of groceries to the top of the tricycle and then I got in behind Jeffrey. We were off.

'What's good, Dong?'

'Ah, same old, nothing new,' I laughingly replied.

He smiled. 'Where do you buy now?'

'Used to be from Felix. These days Buldan scores outside.'

'Oy, Felix no good any more?'

'Son of a bitch always has Botong and his dickless troop hanging at his place.'

'Eh, those retards don't have any money to score anyways! Felix best not hold it against you guys.'

'That ain't it . . . And you, what's up at Butsok's?'

'Ahhh, eh, I was just going to hand over my wife's Avon orders to Ate Rosa.'

'Oh, okay and how's Esmi?'

'She's gone crazy over her American chatmate. Gallant, looks like a celebrity.' His tone got a shade forlorn.

'Wow, where did they meet?'

'Pudring's cybersex. Am sure it's nothing new to you.'

'That's heavy. Your kids?' I changed gears.

'Sent them to Nanang in the province.'

'How's Butsok anyway?'

'News is he left home.'

'So that's why I haven't seen him recently.'

'He'll sure get it from his dad.'

'Mang Delfin's a piece of old school work, no doubt. Not an addict but acts is worse than one. Fucking hell, I remember we didn't have a day at Butsok's back then when his mom wasn't sporting some new bruise.

'Exactly why Butsok's thankful I did his mother a solid.'

'Solid? Why, what did she owe?'

'Ah . . . N-nothing, that's not . . . At Avon s-she had some hassle . . . Owed something to the missus,' Jeffrey stutteringly explained. We took a turn after Nympha's gulaman drink stall.

Jeffrey slowed down. 'Hey brother I'm going to park here, okay? Over there at Pusa's is too tight, hard to get in or out.'

I got off and offloaded my box of groceries from the tricycle roof.

'I'll get to walking, Jeff. Appreciate the ride,' I thanked him and we high-fived.

'Yeah, yeah, next time!' He hurriedly grabbed a long container from the cab side of the tricycle that looked like where kids kept their battling pet spiders. Must be where he kept the items. I took the circuitous route. The labyrinth of alleys and narrow backstreets that composed the Inners presented many paths that led to one exit.

Plenty of holes to choose from here. This is how the Inners care for those who don't want to be found or are evading certain folks. Like me. Like Buldan and I. Botong and his gang should be deep in their cups at this hour, deep into their usual MO of torturing those they knew wouldn't fight back.

Buldan was asleep when I got back.

He had a blanket over his head so I tapped his leg. 'Ey Dan, you eaten yet? Siomai, oy,' I offered. No movement. Why he's under a blanket when the heat can kill is beyond me. Likely high again.

'Dan, that thing I wanted you to buy, you got it?'

'On the small table, Dong,' his voice was muffled under the blanket.

'Thought you were asleep. You smoked up yeah, no?' I said.

The small plastic bag had smears of something wet on it. Trying to make out what I was I sniffed. Smelled like rust, oily. Blood. These are blood stains. I stepped to the rickety, bug-infested bed made from rags and thrown-together driftwood and grabbed Buldan's blanket, hauling it off him. His face was a wreck. Eyebrows shredded, flesh around the eyes puffy and inflamed, his arms gashed from the beating.

'Botong?' I asked. I tried to catch my breath and calm down.

Buldan nodded.

'Didn't give him any?' I added, and he shook his head now.

'How much he want?'

'He wanted the necklace,' Buldan replied.

I didn't know what to say.

'Eat the siomai. I'll buy Red Horse.'

Buldan limped half-awake to where I had left the siomai dumplings. I went out, pocketing the blood-stained plastic bag as I headed out back, a route that took me away from Aling Supreng's where Botong and his gang hung out. I'd buy outside.

Once I was headed out, I surveyed the situation. Botong's feral kids were scattered like goat shit everywhere here in the Inners. Inutile fucks who didn't have anything better to do except hassle others, trash someone else's trip, and swaggeringly display the false bravery they'd acquired from alcohol, meth, and angst. Eyes were on me all the way out, but I walked on, feigning indifference.

I reached Aling Goring's without difficulty, bought two Red Horse mucho bottles and a small Stallion beer. I opened and downed the Stallion until I'd drunk half. Went back to the Inners. I chose a route that put me on a course to pass directly in front of Aling Supreng's store.

Fuck you, Botong. Think you're always going to be the shit in here? Not today, asshole.

Nearing the store, the cackling and guffaws of the bastards grew louder. I could not unsee Buldan's smashed face. *Fuck your mother, Botong, you filth, you swine!* My knees shook. I could feel the fear crawling up my guts to my chest and back down my stomach and up to my head.

Must've been the speed of my pace but I didn't realize I'd already passed Aling Supreng's until someone psssstd at me, calling my attention. I didn't look back.

'Dodong! Hoy!' This one had a big voice. I kept on walking.

Next, I heard even louder laughs and teasing. My senses felt like they were only focused on the drunks.

'DODONG!' was followed by loud thumps of flip-flops. Botong had followed and was behind me. 'You deaf?' He grabbed my arm and as I turned, I swatted his hand away.

'What's your problem?' I sniped.

'Ahhhh, sonova . . . Dodong's brave now, ey?' He looked back at his gang.

'Grab his ear, 'Tong!' Shouted someone from the drinking table.

'I don't have time for this. What the hell do you want?'

'You're not new here, Dong. You know we're all brothers and sisters here in the Inners, right? Just add something to the collection.'

'Pass. I got nothing on me.'

'How'd you buy that, then?' His lips puckered to my beers. 'Don't make us seem like fools.'

'Only had enough for the beers but frisk me all you want,' I said with a hard tone.

The bastard actually patted me down. My jeans almost fell down and not even the garter on my briefs was spared.

'Swallowed the money, did you, Dong?' His eyes widened and laughed then followed it up with an even louder cackle from his drinking buddies. 'But your friend had plenty of cash, unlike you.'

I said under my breath, 'cause he knew how to make some.'

'Say what?'

'Nothing . . .'

'Guess we'll just settle for those beers, then, Dong.'

'Two muchos are all that's in here, Botong. Catch you next time.'

He suddenly grabbed my arm and put his face against mine. 'You son of a whore, you've been dicking me around and embarrassing me in front my friends. Pretending to be deaf when I'm calling you? Consider yourself lucky I didn't smack you right away. You're making a fuss over two beers?'

'Two's all I got. They're to help me sleep,' I reasoned, wiping his spit from my face.

'Sleep? You want to get lined up to sleep as rough as Buldan?'

Darkness settled around my peripheral vision.

'Here. Go take it all,' I brusquely handed both the beers from the plastic. Botong grabbed them, passed them on to someone from the drinking table.

'Such an unnecessary waste of time.' Then he let go of my arm. I turned around and walked off, with only the Stallion bottle in my hand to show for my time at the store.

'Psssst! Dong! You forgot!' Botong shouted after me.

I stopped in my tracks and looked back. His lips pointed at the Stallion bottle.

'Donate that as well.' He walked towards me.

'Botong, I could've given you change too if you'd only told me to buy you beer with my money.' I handed him the last bottle.

'You're such a joker, Dodong!' He laughed. 'Never you mind, tonight you just rest, you know they do warn against too much drinking being bad for your health.'

'Forget anything else, like maybe my briefs? This one has gold lining inside you can maybe pawn.'

'Nah, my pet python here would never fit such small undies,' he announced, followed by approving laughter form his drinking colleagues. 'But we appreciate these donations!'

'You're welcome and may there be many people who pass you by with beer, so you guys never run out.'

'You nailed it! Let's high-five on that.' We actually did clap on it and the bastard regarded the Stallion bottle in his hand, holding it up to eye level and seeing that it was still almost full to the brim.

'Well, it looks like you hardly drank anything here. It would be a shame if you didn't stay and have a few rounds?' He teased.

'Am good. Had one at Butsok's. That's all yours.'

'If you say so,' he shrugged and walked back to the table, taking swigs as he did.

I continued walking back to the room. All cleaned out.

I did, however, bring a smile back with me. I hope Che likes the necklace. I'll just clean it with vinegar, I guess. I flicked the creased plastic bag into the canal.

6

Bursting into the room, Dodong straight away turned off all the white lights and left the yellow ones on. He jumped Che, attacking her with kisses. His right hand grabbed her breasts, the other cupped her generous ass. In return, Che pushed down his jeans and caressed his cock, already wet on its tip with anticipation.

Che hurried downstairs following an exchange of saliva and took Dodong's cock into her mouth, pleasuring it like a lollipop. Dodong's body writhed in unexplainable joy with each motion of her tongue. Like a combo of a calmative injected into his bloodstream and too many packets of Extra Joss energy drink. With his right hand, he gently stroked the top of Che's head while nudging his groin into her mouth, his balls throbbing with added intensity with each ingress. His left hand held her left breast in a gentle squeeze.

When he felt close to bursting, he pulled out from her mouth and raised Che up from her knees. He laid her down to the bed, raining kisses on her neck slowly with his arms behind her.

Gentle kisses were traced from her neck to her breasts and down to her belly button. With the power of his tongue and lips he made her moan until, finally, he arrived at his desired destination. As a preamble, he whetted his appetite by sniffing and giving pecking smacks to her pussy.

A deeper yet still angelic moan resonated through the room, motivating Dodong to move shrewdly with his tongue. His target was the pearl among the folds. Plainly visible, it was there, throbbing in that territory between her asshole and pussy.

When Che's ululations sounded like she was in total delirium he inserted his middle finger, adding its motion to his tongue's ministrations. He continued to press his finger inward until he felt the part that was textured like a sponge. Pressing against that coarseness, he appreciated the sight of Che writhing and quivering, like she didn't know what to do with herself.

'Dong, have mercy and put it in, please Dong!' She shouted.

Exhilarating, those words. Still, he only surfaced for air when Che's knees began to tremble, knocking against each other. She opened wide. Her legs welcomed Dodong as he positioned himself for a slow entry, his tip massaging the opening to further their excitement. Leisurely, he went in.

'Sonovabitch, Che! Ahhhhrghhg!'

'Dong! Uhgrhhhgh!'

His thrusts were slow, yet powerful. Che held on to him like her life depended on it. She added her fingers to the wonderful mess, massaging her clit in time to his thrusts.

'Deeper now, Dong!'

Dodong took hold of the headboard, using it for leverage to grind all the way into Che. Her fingers went faster and faster, circling her clit in a circular polishing motion. Balls deep in her, pelvic bone against pelvic bone, he felt his climax welling up once more.

Dodong refused to finish. He pulled out. Che turned around, her ass in the air. Dodong wasted no time and went in again. His lizard brain making him drive relentlessly into the beauty of Che's curved waist, a bend that arced into a smooth, perfectly round ass. They took their sweet time in this position.

'Lie down, Dong,' she called out, turning her head from the bed to look at him pleading.

A couple more thrusts before he obeyed and pulled out. He had barely laid down when Che was already on top of him, then he was in and her softness wrapped his cock. From his vantage, he could see more of her, all of her.

Faster and faster went Che's hips riding Dodong to her heart's content. Fingers on her clit matched the corkscrew motion. Moans and sighs were their only language. Sounds full of yearning and elation. They might not have been able to form coherent words, but their noises were an intimate conversation meant only for the two of them.

'Doooong! I'm so close, Dooong! Ugh!'

'Wait for me, Cheeeee! Ughmmrh!'

'Sonova . . . Ughmmm!'

'Ahghhh!'

'Ahhummgghm . . . hmm . . . '

Che laid her cheek on Dodong's sweaty chest. He stroked her hair, damp with perspiration as well.

'I love you so much, Che,' he blurted out.

'I am so afraid, Dong.'

Dodong thought, *So am I.* Yet he could only say, searching as he was for a good response, 'We'll get past this, Che.'

'My nights can be so long. He doesn't let me sleep. He's even my nightmares.'

'More threats?'

'Nothing more for us to hide, Dong. He knows everything. Even Mayet's been dragged into it, too. This is all we have.'

'We can go home to Bicol. And then stay put. He'll never be able to track us down there.'

'Elmer's got connections everywhere. He knows people in the police and the syndicates. It's wishful thinking he wouldn't be able to track us down. Sometimes I'm afraid to even step out there. There's a feeling he's just around a corner. Watching us, watching everything.' Che hugged him tighter.

'My fears have overtaken me,' she said, her lips trembling.

'Fuck him! Fuck that son of a whore! It's only his position that makes him brave, protecting him from whatever we can do!'

'That's my point. Who can we run to? Who do we tell? He might as well be the law.'

'I'll find a way. Let me worry about that,' he reassured Che.

'I don't want to get my hopes dashed. Only thing I ask of you, Dong, is that you don't leave me. The kids, Dong. If anything happens, you must be there to care for them.'

'Why talk like that, Che?'

'Because, Dong, I know Elmer. I know him better than you do, and I know what that animal is capable of.'

What could he say then? His only reply was a giant kiss on her lips and a tight embrace. He got up, took his jeans from the floor, feeling for something in the pocket. Finding the folded piece of paper, he drew it out.

'Come, Che.'

'Why, Dong?'

'*Basta*, please come here.'

Che got up. They both faced the mirror. Dodong kissed Che on the nape and the back.

'Please put up your hair.' She obeyed though she was puzzled. From the folded piece of white paper he revealed the necklace. Che saw it from the mirror. And they both smiled.

7

Two in the morning and everyone's awake except for the man in the coffin. People have broken off into their own clusters according to activity; in prayer, over beers, flirting, singing videoke, and the almighty petty gambling.

When visitors arrived you'd hear . . .

'How'd he die?'

'How much did the hospital fees set you back?'

'But I just talked to him recently.'

All were ways to signify one's condolences.

I was getting antsier by the minute, yet there was still no sight of Buldan. Soon enough I'd likely bet my balls. *Cara y cruz* was utterly demonic in its addictiveness, so much so that it's capable of buying your soul.

Sayeth the demon: entrust your fate to a power above us all—chance, which none hold sway over.

'Kara!' Maykel shrilly declared his win.

Sonova . . . Rage quitting was now imminent. Whore's son piss and shit. 700 pesos down the drain. Goddamn your fucking mother. Good thing I didn't bring everything I had with me. I knew this story well. Gambler's sickness is what it is. Incapability to accept loss. Keep on firing while there's still ammo. And even without bullets, you'd try to loan your liver for just a few more flips of the coin. Not me, no sir. Everyone at the table knew this was how every brawl started. Not tonight. No way. At a wake? C'mon, that would be utterly embarrassing.

'What now, Dong?' Maykel asked.

'Am out. Too salty for me.'

'Buldan around?'

'Nowhere to be found and still hasn't come home. Bet you a truck hit the fucker.'

Maykel laughed. 'You crazy. Get yourself some coffee.'

'Yeah, I'll get back my 700 with tons of coffee 'til I squirm like a caffeinated worm,' I said, to which Maykel dutifully laughed loudly. Bit too hard, maybe. I took a place beside the people in prayer, sat down and regarded the coffin. Other than those with a terminal illness, might there be people who've prepared themselves for their passing? I'd still put money on a big part of the terminally sick populace believing they'd live on contrary to all the medical predictions. Hoping 'til the very end.

'Yet our life is not ours, all things go back to Him, all is surrendered to Him, and God shall bless his soul,' chorused the people in prayer.

I wanted to retort, 'Well, if that's the case I'll go ahead and go out on my own terms thank you very much. Just think about it. You're born to learn how to live, then it's just cut off after you took all that time educating yourself on its intricacies? No whore's son is going to catch me alive. Even Him. No damn way, friend.'

'Let us repent while we are on earth so that at the end of our lives, heaven shall be within our reach,' they added.

Heaven within our reach? I'd bet once again that, even if folks really truly wanted to hang out in heaven, nobody wanted to die just to get there.

'He was still so young. What a tragedy,' whispered an old woman behind me to the senior man with eyes closed beside her. Well, all those people who died young and yet were buried only when they were already shrivelled like a vegetable left in the sun might have something to say about that.

What I mean is, here in the Inners, for example, it's a never-ending inside peek into the gears and cogs of death. We're all fucking dead down here. Only thing we can't predict is when we'll be six feet under. None of us have the inside scoop on that, yet we know full well that death isn't just measured by getting shipped out in a box. Even with gambling and prayer, we keep vigil at our own wakes on the daily. Because we die every day. With every neighbourhood in this country that's like the Inners, death carries absolutely no mystery.

Aaaah, such a life. Likely why it pains us to lose someone or to even think of dying. We have way too many treasured memories to hold on to, good and bad. Unlike mosquitoes. One slap and that's all she wrote. No memory to take with it or to leave behind, remembered only by the swelling of its bite on your arm and the bloody smear on your palm.

'Pssssst' said someone behind me.

When I turned my head, it was Buldan. I stood and walked to him. 'Where've you been and what took you so long? Loan me 700 now,' I greeted him.

'Who the heck is Francisco Dela Luna?' He asked, trying to catch his breath.

'C'mon, you don't know?'

'Eh, I wouldn't have asked if I goddamn did,' he retorted.

I slung my arm over Buldan's shoulder and guided him slowly to the front of the wake, so we could view the face within the open casket.

'There, that's Francisco Dela Luna.'

Buldan's eyes widened into saucers. I left him gawking at the coffin and went back to my seat. Fucker couldn't believe it. He regarded the face inside that coffin for long minutes. I watched him watching the dead guy. After a while a woman in a duster, wide and old, approached Buldan with eyes puffy from weeping. Aling Perla. She gently caressed Buldan on the back.

'Buldan, whatever Botong did to you, I hope you can find it in your heart to forgive my son's sins,' she sobbingly petitioned.

Buldan asked, 'How did he die, mother?'

'They were all drinking over at Supleng's, then one of his friends said he just . . . keeled over. He started shaking like an epileptic and his mouth foamed.'

Buldan turned to look at me and sighed. I lit a cigarette. Buldan was struggling not to smile, I could tell.

8

Neither Che nor Mayet had come out and he was almost fit to burst from all the fishballs and kikiam minced pork sausage he'd eaten. He hadn't heard anything from the two girls since yesterday. Maybe Elmer still had eyes on them both and didn't want to risk it?

'Mang Rey,' he asked the fishball cart vendor, 'Either of our girls come out since this morning?'

'Sorry son, I haven't noticed at all.'

'How about Elmer, he come out?'

'Didn't even see him come in.'

'Ahhhh . . .'

'I got to piss, Dong. Watch the cart for a bit will you,' Mang Rey said, making a beeline for a shadowy corner.

'Go ahead.'

When Mang Rey was out of sight Dodong hurriedly speared fishballs from the frying pan and devoured them, huffing his mouth since they were still too hot. When he'd eaten all the ones in the wok, he took a new bag of fish balls from the small cabinet underneath and laid out a fresh batch in the pan. They cooked quickly enough. Just as they turned golden brown Dodong speared them, so impatient for them to cool down that he almost choked from everything he was chewing. He didn't even notice Mang Rey come back until the old man was already beside him. He swallowed everything in his bulging mouth, chewed or not.

'Well, that was fast,' he cheerfully greeted the vendor.

'Dong . . .' Mang Rey drew close and whispered.

'Oh?'

'Che is at the Caltex gas station. The girl's comfort room,' Mang Rey said, his voice still low.

Dodong stopped in his tracks and hurriedly filched for change to pay Mang Rey.

'I'll pay you the rest tomorrow for sure. Thank you, Mang Rey!' He walked swiftly to the gas station nearby, just two corners from Karuza, the bounce in his step a sign of his anticipation to see Che again.

When he got to Caltex, Dodong made a beeline for the women's and stood outside the door. He whistled three times. Moments later someone walloped him from behind. The force of the blow to his head made him bend over. It was followed by a punch that made him see silver lights. The pain sent him to his knees. He was dizzy and his legs wobbled even as he tried to regain his senses. The last thing he heard was a heavy thud before everything went black.

He came to only to be assaulted by a filthy toilet paired reeking of piss and shit that seemed to have been pickled in the summer heat for days. No idea where he'd been taken. Dodong was sprawled on a floor blanketed by urine, phlegm, and murky, odious waters flowing out from rusted pipes. A kick to the face put him down again as he tried to rise. He fell facedown and his cheek kissed the grimy, broken tiles. Red blotches from his nose added to the soupy mess on the floor.

The same man who'd kicked him grabbed his hair and stood him up against the wall in front of the toilet.

'How are things, you son of a whore?'

Between puffy lids, Dodong tried to make out the face in front of him. He could only discern four big men, blob-like shapes to his injured sight and the blinking bulb in the toilet. He couldn't place these thugs, from what little he could see of their faces.

'Don't know me, ha?' Another heavy kick from his captor to the chest.

Blood spewed from Dodong's mouth. 'N-no . . . What did I do, chief?'

'Eh, fucking comedian here with hilarious jokes,' said the man with another kick, this time to the face. Heavier than the last.

'AWGHugh!' The heel of the man's boots left an imprint on Dodong's cheek. 'B-Boss, show mercy p-please . . . I don't know what offence I made but I'll make it up to you, boss,' he begged even as the pain hit him.

'Boss, guy says he didn't do anything,' seconded one of the thugs.

'Tell me, if a woman fights back, is her pussy doubly delicious? Tell me how nice it must be,' said the man beating him.

'B-Boss? I d-don't know a-anything, please,' Dodong insisted.

'Must be exciting to fuck in the middle of all that talahib grass, ha? Tall grass and open air are a thrill.' The man grabbed Dodong's hair again and smashed the back of his head against the wall. Blood marked in splatter lines across the broken tiles from his fresh wound.

By this time the strength to advocate on his behalf had turned to vapour. He felt his jaw loosening, like it was about to get unscrewed and fall to the filthy floor along with his waning consciousness. The words 'fuck' and 'grass' and 'stab' kept droning from the thugs.

'SON OF A WHORE! YOU RAPED CHE! YOU ANIMAL!'

The man's shout echoed through every corner of the small bathroom. 'YOU KILLED CHE-CHE, GODDAMNED SON OF A BITCH!' The thug smashed his head once more against the wall. More blood flowed from the same wound.

His senses distanced themselves from the wounds and the weight of all the blows he'd received. Something pulled his consciousness out of its delirium when he heard the name of his beloved from the lips of the thugs around him.

'B-Boss? Chieeef? I d-don't know a-anyone named C-Che.'

'Ahh? Acting now are we, you fuckface?' Grabbed by his hair, the thug moved Dodong from the wall, another of the gang assisting him with the dead weight.

'B-Boss, please please f-forgive me, have mercy sir -bbb-bo-blllblbbbbbbrbbbsh!' Dodong's speech as cut short by his head getting dunked in the toilet water.

As his brain filed this moment into its cortex, Dodong's memory would forever be sharply marked as he tasted the uniquely singular flavour of pickled shit and piss in the rotting toilet of precinct nine.

When they raised his head from the depths of the toilet bowl, he felt something kind of soft, kind of hard inside his mouth. It almost went down his throat. Just a bit deeper and he'd have swallowed it already. His gag reflex kicked in. Fortunately, he coughed out the object with a mighty spew. There on the floor was a *tubol*—hardened crap the shape of a short sausage. Like a breakfast longganisa in varying shades of brown and black. His vomit followed the oblong-shaped tubol with a broth of blood and stomach acid. Bits of rice and half-chewed fishballs from Mang Rey came up too, garnish to the stew.

'Pick that shit up, whore's son!' The man standing above him ordered.

He continued to spit out blood. Only Che's voice was in his ears. 'I'm so afraid, Dong', yet he was far, far away from the punches, kicks, and strikes he was being dealt. Dodong felt nothing.

'Sonovabitch, not going to pick that up?'

'Boss, fucker is a tough one oh? Playing deaf now!'

'Give him a shot. Guaranteed it'll bring him back to reality.'

One of the thugs pulled out his pistol. Cocked it. Pointed the cold barrel against Dodong's temple. Nothing from Dodong. Instead, he continued to beg, 'Sirs, please, boss, you have to believe me.'

'Bastard!'

'Think we're idiots? Ha?'

'Pick up that thing!'

BANG!

The gunshot to the ceiling made the ancient cobwebs tremble and fall. The sound brought Dodong back to the present situation. They all laughed as he started shivering, the shock to his system was no different than a poisoned rat writhing in agony.

'Whoreson, pick it up!'

He hurriedly picked up the tubol from the floor. The crap had hardened so much that it had still retained its shape despite being on the wet floor. It was slippery in his hands. Like newly caught fish.

'Eat it,' the thug ordered, gun pointed at Dodong's bleeding face.

Dodong couldn't imagine how things had gotten this dire. That he was now being forced to swallow somebody else's shit. He couldn't even conceive of eating his own poop.

'Not going to eat that, ha?' The gun pressed hard against his head. 'You guys might want to step back. Beware, this fool might spew on us,' the gunman reminded his friends.

Dodong envisioned the alternate path where his brains would be what was splattered on the walls if he didn't eat the damn thing.

BANG!

Another shot rang out, this time hitting the rim of the toilet beside him. The commode's contents splattered around the cubicle. Pieces of shit stuck to the walls. Shaken, Dodong hurriedly put the tubol in his mouth.

'You best not swallow yet. Chew on that.'

Dodong chomped on the hardened crap like it was day old chewing gum. The tears streaming down both of his cheeks weren't for him, he reasoned. They were for Che and her wretched fate. Staring at the muck on the floor, his senses might be numb but neither was his mind nor his memory. A laughing man standing above him was reflected on all the wetness.

This was the thug who had reduced his world to a prison, the culprit behind Che's bruises and gashes, the callouses on her vagina. And now, his suspicions raised, the obvious perpetrator of his beloved's murder; a crime being pinned on him. He was the thug who owned the law round these parts: Elmer.

9

Well, I can't move my arms. Blinking makes my face ache. My whole body's like a broadcast signal for my impotence. Che's gone. Couldn't do anything about it. Somewhere, deep down in my bones, I just knew it would all come to this. Yet I always held out hope that chance would favour us one day, grant us escape.

Humans are a selfish species. I foolishly trusted luck, forgot to wrestle down my own senseless rationale. I was . . . I am a coward for inclining towards a better tomorrow, despite conditions that were appallingly contrary. The best possible outcome in my mind was that Elmer would one day tire of Che. That our happy ending would come in the aftermath, and we would achieve escape velocity. We would then finally be free to be together. Why did I let the talisman of favourable destiny carry something so important? I did nothing but wait, wait, wait, meanwhile Che was betting her life just to keep the status quo, to keep us, keep me, a secret.

And as I waited for Elmer to tire of my beloved, he had seized the chance to end it all according to his own design. Che's execution was a clean slice that broke him from being a suspect. In one stroke he made sure nobody else could have her, so I wouldn't be able to love her, so he didn't have to face his own brutishness. Most of all so that he could keep his hands and image as an upstanding policeman fucking clean as a whistle. His barbarism was now pinned on me.

No idea why Elmer and his posse didn't finish me when they had the chance. For sure it was not out of pity. Likely, there were more humiliations in store for me later on in this gruesome show. From what I heard, they said I would need to be placed under investigation. After all the animalism they had perpetrated on me, they'll have me investigated? Dig up the stink that I call my life after I had already accepted my fate? There's a cold logic to it, I must admit. This way all the documents are clean when they kick me up to Muntinlupa's New Bilibid Prison. Once there, they'd make sure the good old boys would have a fiesta all over my asshole. I'll have no rest until a merciful prolapse rendered me useless.

'Psssst, hoy!' The officer from the desk called to me.

'Is that me, sir?' I asked to make sure.

'Well, no other roach in that cell, eh,' the pig said.

'What can I do for you, sir?' I asked.

'Visitor.'

'Oh, what's his name?'

He picked up the phone and talked to whoever was on the other end. 'Says his name's Volcano, bulkan something?'

'Oh no, sir, he might explode up in here,' I joked.

'Fuckface! You know him or not?'

'Apologies, sir. Yeah, I know him.'

Back on the phone and he was nodding to the voice in the receiver. He went back to working on his typewriter after he ended the conversation.

Escorted by a young rookie police officer in front of him, I saw Buldan enter the police station. The rookie briefed him before they let him see me. Said briefing included plenty of scolding and talking down to. To his credit, Buldan nodded and took it like a man. When it mercifully ended, Buldan was able to stand outside my cell.

'Dong, who did all that?' He greeted me with a tone of surprise, obviously at my now decimated face and bruised condition.

'Mosquitoes, they're vicious in here,' I joked.

'Dong, I'm serious.'

'One of them was your escort,' I whispered.

'One of them? Well, how many were they?'

'Four. I think.'

'Motherfucker, Dong. Why'd you let them catch you?'

'Idiot, this one's different.'

'Ha?' He said, confused. From between the bars, I put my mouth near his ears.

'They pinned a murder on me.'

'Shit, who got killed?'

'Keep your damn voice down. I'm the one got beat up in here and you're the one getting spooked.'

'Dong, who was it? You know the victim?' He asked.

'It was Che.'

'Che who?'

'My girl, the one who works at Red Butterfly.'

'The fuck happened?'

'Raped her. Stabbed her,' I didn't try to stop the tear running down my cheek. Buldan could only express his bewilderment with wrinkled brows.

'Those sons of bitches! Dong, how can they even accuse you of that?'

'Long story, Buldan.'

'What do we do, Dong. How much is the bail?'

'No idea, don't even try to bail me out. Sure bet Elmer won't let that happen.'

'Dong, who's Elmer?'

'Ah, just trust me.'

'Well, what do I do, Dong, tell me?'

It was clear that Buldan was worried to bits about me, scared for me too. I grabbed his shirt and pressed his face close to the bars so I could be sure only he would hear what I had to say.

'Listen, you know that poster of Glydel Mercado beside the cabinet. Behind that is a small cubby for my things. Open that and inside should be a biscuit container, it's round and made of tin. Che's letters and pictures are inside plus two teabags of *ganja* and some leftover shabu. Clean all of it. Burn the photos. Burn all the drug items.'

'Alright, Dong.'

'I told them I didn't know Che.'

'Sooo they'll be dropping by the room, Dong?'

'That's why I'm telling you to clean it all up.'

'Okay Dong, That's what I'll do. I'll clean everything. Okay, clean it up, no problem.'

The young rookie came back to bring Buldan out. I tapped my friend's shoulder to give him some comfort that everything will turn out alright.

'Escort's here. You'll have to go.'

'I'll come back tomorrow, Dong.'

'You take care.'

'Back at you, Dong!'

With Buldan being led out of the jail I went and sat in a part of the cell that was dim and shadowed. I wanted no brightness right now.

10

Buldan was orphaned in 2006. The murderer of his family was one of the innumerable fires that ravaged the shanties and ghettos of the Inners with some regularity. He had come home from scavenging the trash heaps to the shock of several fire trucks parked outside the only road leading to their ramshackle homes. He pushed through the throng. As Buldan made his way through the thick crowd of rubberneckers and residents, coming the other way was none other than Andoy—veteran junkie and his mother's boyfriend—who wasted no time telling Buldan that among the victims of the blaze were his mom and three sisters.

No reaction marred Buldan's face. No trace of distress nor surprise. Something inside him rejoiced. This turn of events really was for the best. The suffering of his three sisters was at least over now. Part of what the fire claimed was his sisters' memories of Andoy's rape. The nightmare of his clockwork violations.

Three days later, Andoy was found dead on the doorstep of his new girlfriend's house. A rusty ball bearing in his neck was the cause of death, the kind fired from a makeshift prison firearm popularly known as a '*sumpak*'.

***

The small hours of the early morning and I was woken up by the ruckus of a police baton rattling against the steel bars.

'Up in there, hoy!' Said the pig, continuing to bang his baton against my cell.

I stood. He unlocked my door. Opened the cell. The baton was still banging against steel, the sound delivering heavy fear to my guts with each beat.

'Your back to me, boy,' he ordered.

I heard the clink of handcuffs. I turned and he cuffed my arms behind me. His heavy hands surely left bruises on my wrists. He walked me out in front of him.

***

For a few months, Buldan busied himself with scavenging the trash and bringing anything of value to the recyclers. His wanderings brought along with it the start of a regular drug habit. Starting small, he sniffed sealant, particularly the Vulca Seal sold in cheap dimebags by the Chinese merchant Mi Xang. Thing was, the spirit of Vulca Seal lasted longer in his brain than any calories soup or rice could provide. It was all his 5 pesos could afford.

Some nights he'd hang out with a band of feral street teens and kids who had made an abandoned building in Bictuan their headquarters. Without adults or authority around, they were free to inhale all the rugby and sealant they wanted. It wasn't all highs from household chemicals. Buldan also got to know Penpen, God's burnt creation and the sole girl among them. She was also the gang's default cumbucket. Buldan tasted all of her with eagerness. One time, when he was in the middle of eating her out, an insect bit his lip. The bite quickly grew red and inflamed. He swore never to go down on Penpen again. Those pubic lice were nasty.

* * *

They brought me to the parking lot where a Toyota VIOS waited. Elmer was there with his police friends, laughing at something.

'Look who's here now.'

They stopped me before I got into the car. Layers of cloth were tied around my eyes as a blindfold. They must not want me to see the animalism they'd perpetrate on my poor soul soon. Such merciful police.

We drove out of the parking lot. Without sight, I tried to activate my hearing and sense of smell. Lighters clicked as we started our trip.

'Cortez best keep that window closed.'

Fuckers kept lighting up meth despite the bumpy drive.

'Now how do we get to this Dreamland?'

My guts were sounding alarms. I kept quiet.

A warm fist greeted the right side of my face. The part that was still swollen from my previous beating. The strength of it off-balanced me, making me lie down on my left side.

'Cortez, motherfucker. You stand down!' The guy on my left tossed me back to a sitting position.

'Want to tell me where this Dreamland is?' Asked the guy to my right again.

'Behind the new Camella subdivision,' I finally said.

'Shithead!' Another punch came, this time from the left. My jaw wobbled now. Along with the metallic taste—definitely a cut on the inside of my mouth—were the salty taste of tears from the hurt and ache of all the hits I'd taken. I couldn't stop them from falling.

'Son of a whore, where is Dreamland?'

* * *

Buldan didn't stay long and departed the building of the young ferals to be a nomad on his own. How could he not go? Penpen got pregnant and, since there was absolutely no way they could fuck her, the boys wanted to substitute him for her to slake their depravity. It was better to be a legitimate loner.

It took some doing but he finally landed a job as a collector of discarded soft drink bottles and plastics. The junk shop in the Inners, where he delivered his collection, was near his old house. Buldan was no longer a good-for-nothing curbside loafer, instead he could proudly parade a wooden pushcart with inspirational words scrawled bold and large on the side declaring: ONLY GOD CAN'T JUDS ME +++ RIL TAGS.

Buldan's finances levelled up. The 5-peso daily wage shot up to 20 pesos. He turned to the salving oblivion of Vulca Seal less and less. He was able to afford vegetable spring rolls—the lumpiang toge that was the national merienda in the Inners. Did you think it was Lucky Me pancit canton noodles? Then dust motes have more logic than your bourgeoisie deduction.

* * *

I can still remember Che telling me that Elmer's connections ran so wide that he practically knew everything. Yet this gang of pigs are beating me up now just for Dreamland's location.

'Ey chief, the fishball vendor said it's near the soap factory,' said the guy riding up front. He's right, of course.

'Oy, you smegma. Didn't you say it was behind Camella?' Said the guy to my right.

I stayed quiet, waiting for a hit to the head. When it came, I almost spat out my soul. 'Ughhgh!' The air left my lungs since they hit me in the solar plexus, just when I was expecting it to my head.

'Hoy, you son of a whore. Listen up. You know where we're going now so if you try and fool us again you might not make it to your house,' added the guy to my right.

I was ready to die the night they told me how Che had gone. Proof that Elmer had no balls. Then again, trying to disguise Che's murder and fob it on someone else made sense since he was connected to my girl. It wasn't just any connection either. Every pig in the operating district knew he was a suspect. The modus of an early move to takeout Che was just perfect. He executed the play so that he could put up the masquerade of an investigation, cover the evil he had committed, and still have his hands clean. Plus, it made it look like he was working the case at the same time. Which brings poor old me to this moment. Servile sheep to this gang of pigs. Hell, even we urban poor creatures who live in the Inners without any kind of education have the ability to think. It was just luck that it was these bastards the government chose to arm, swinging their swaggering corruption like administration-approved dicks as they got more and more drunk on power. After generations of their filth, where are we? Prohibited from saying what we think.

Especially anything that might disadvantage them. And who can say anything good about them, anyway? Not a booger's amount of charitable acts. Silence is the result. Be quiet or get lead in the head.

I just hope Buldan can clean up my shit before we get there. Maybe the car will get into a horrific crash in the meantime?

'I urge you to stop this shit, ha? Help us help you. I just need one answer for every question. Trust me, we will know if you're telling the truth or fucking with us. Understand?'

I nodded. Let's see what happens.

* * *

One afternoon, Buldan was coming home from collecting junk all over the neighbourhood when a man, running, suddenly dove into his pushcart. The man begged Buldan to hide him. Said some bad mofos were after him. Buldan hurriedly covered the man with pieces of cardboard, old newspapers, and empty sacks of rice. Eventually, three guys came running from the same direction. They were uniformed police. It was at that point that he realized who and what he had hidden in his pushcart.

When the police had disappeared and after good distance, Buldan went to Mang Max's grillery. The man came out of the cart and thanked him profusely. In return, the man bought Buldan several spring rolls.

Buldan knew criminal moves when he saw it, yet he was still curious enough to ask the man why the police were after him. He was a hold-upper, the man replied without hesitation. Next came a confession. He and his partner's latest jeepney robbery had gone horribly sideways. Turned out one of the passengers was a plain clothes police officer. Said police officer was hence able to quickly contact the neighbourhood cops on duty. Plainclothes guy shot the man's partner in the foot. Armed only with knives, they were literally outgunned. The only option the man saw was to make a run for it. When the sound of approaching sirens rang in the air, it cemented his fear and motivation to survive, leaving his wounded partner behind.

* * *

The cop in the passenger seat cracked his window open. I heard the lighter click again. First came the smell of an ordinary cigarette, then the robustness of laundry detergent followed. We were almost at Dreamland. My heart rate jumped ten times faster. If I was really unlucky, not only would Buldan not have cleaned anything, these pigs would burst in on him smoking gak.

'I see the factory, boss.'

'Oy, you pubic strand, we're just about there. Remember: one answer for one question, alright? Make this fast, no leading us around. Getting us tired will make us cranky and you surely don't want us cranky.'

'*Opo*. Yes, sir,' I answered.

* * *

The conversation had meandered to the unique experiences the man had had while engaging in criminal activity. The lucky, the early, and the fast earners. Something tickled the back of Buldan's mind as the robber continued his stories. He realized this marauder of jeepneys had started to trust him.

Buldan eventually suggested he might go with the man on one of his robbery attempts. He wanted to see, he confessed, if he had the balls for such a life. The man refused. Buldan countered with the 'but I saved your life' card, sweetened by the suggestion that Buldan might inform on him, telling the police where he'd gone. But the robber stood firm. He reasoned that he didn't really know Buldan at all and, according to his quick assessment, it was very likely he wouldn't make a good crook with his weak mind and lacklustre ingenuity. Buldan, disappointed, bid the robber a good night and left. He hadn't eaten a single bite of the spring rolls.

* * *

They parked the van outside the soap factory, a block from Dreamland. A weight lifted off the seat beside me. The demons got off one by one. Ah, a few seconds of peace.

Someone from my left side then yanked me out the door. I almost fell to the asphalt but regained my footing. We started to walk. Someone beside me held me up by my arm, guiding and prodding.

'Your visitor earlier, who was he?' This question came from the voice that had been up front in the vehicle.

'Neighbour,' I said.

'Think we're idiots?'

'Maybe you think we don't know you gave instructions to your friend, the one who doesn't like to bathe?' The guy behind me said.

I thought my chest would explode, my bowels erupting from all the anxiety. I kept quiet. We kept on walking until we came to the entrance to Dreamland.

'We're here, boy. We don't want any more runarounds, ha? Give your neighbours some shame and a good night's sleep. You wouldn't want them to wake up in the middle of the night and see someone's brains draining into the gutter.'

'Y-yes sir.'

And we went into the Inners. Each step made my knees weak and my gait wobbly.

'We're at a fork. Now, do we go left or right?'

'Left . . .'

* * *

As Buldan was pushing the cart towards the junk shop, he suddenly felt someone drape an arm around him and the cold hardness of a blade was pressed to his side. The pushcart stopped. He turned towards the thief and recognized him. It was the man who had hid in his cart. The robber put the knife away and, putting his arms up, mimed that it was all just a joke. Buldan's face held no trace of amusement.

'I told you, this job's not for you,' chided the man.

'Oh, eh, why'd you even bother running after me, idiot?' Buldan replied.

The man explained that he was also looking for a place, maybe a room to rent. Where he had been staying was understandably hot right now after his botched jeepney hold-up.

'Yeah, I know a place,' Buldan said.

'Sounds great, come check it out with me,' the man petitioned.

'Eh, didn't you just tell me you didn't want me on your excursions?' Buldan told the robber, who fell silent at his words being thrown back at him.

'Motherfucker, fine, fine. Go park your cart at the junk shop. If you can find me a decent room, I'll bring you along on some of my jobs,' the man relented.

'Deal!'

Inside, Buldan was rejoicing. He went to the junk shop and returned his pushcart, then he fetched the man and they both went to Mang Max's room to let.

* * *

Quickly he ripped down Glydel's poster and behind it was taped a piece of cardboard for Zesto juice drink that hid the small hole. They'd been staying for a pretty long time in the room, yet Buldan never thought that there was even a hole behind the sexy star. Within the hole was the small biscuit can. Grabbing the can, he put it beside his ear and shook.

* * *

Walking for around fifteen minutes and I had no idea how long I could hoodwink these pigs, leading them to nowhere.

'Son of a bitch, boss, we've been walking in circles,' one of the police told Elmer.

'Left, right, or straight ahead?' Elmer asked me.

'Right,' I replied.

'Best be sure,' Elmer said.

'I'm sure.' Just shoot me, sons of whores!

We'd stopped. My blindfold was taken off. We were right in front of our room. These clever little gremlins! I was in fucking trouble now.

'Nothing to say eh?'

'Told ya you can't fool us.'

A hard kick to my hips sent me sprawling into a line of buckets. This sent dogs to a chorus of barking.

'Cortez, you braindead fuck, you'll wake the whole ghetto! Be quiet, stupid sonofabitch.'

'Apologies, boss. It's this whoreson's fault, eh.' Cortez mimed kicking me again.

Cortez helped me up. Nothing from Buldan, who must be dead asleep right now. Normally, noise like that would make him peep out our lone window, waiting for a fight so he could watch. Nothing now. This part of the Inners was quiet, too. Only the barking of canines resonated through the narrow alleys.

It was Cortez who kicked down our sorry excuse for a door, made out of wood scraps and an aluminium roof. The hinges broke easy. I was left outside with one of Elmer's minions watching me as they assaulted our room.

'Boss, what the fuck!'

'Tsk! Tsk! Tsk! Shit and hell!'

'Tsk! You! Get that fucker in here,' Elmer peeked out and motioned my minder to bring me in.

He pushed me into the room and immediately I saw Buldan's body sprawled on the floor. My guts churned, I wanted to hurl. My head spun as I noticed how Buldan's mouth was foaming, blood was all over the floor. I felt like the ground was about to meet me when I noticed how his shorts were down around his ankles. His dick was out. It had been cut off. Dismembered, literally. Che's photos were strewn all around. Beside Buldan's head was the silver necklace with a heart pendant. Blood covered it as well. Beside the necklace was a bottle of silver cleaner.

II

The Violence We Are All Heirs To

11

In the morning, Dreamland's filthy basketball court seemed like people were playing the folk game where the flowers opened and closed. The circle ever-widening in tempo to the loudening volume of whispers and banter. The gossipmongers' faces were wrinkled, their noses mashed to palms to combat the rising reek of corpse-scent wafting into the hood with the morning breezes.

'Such a soulless animal that could do that!' Said a crone almost vomiting her words at the sight nobody had forced her to witness.

The siblings Butsok and Myla shook their heads when they passed by the court, smelling the salt and hot reek of bodies pressed together in full rumour-mongering conference. This was nothing new to the brother and sister, same old as they'd say. Only when they went into the throng and saw what everyone was making a ruckus about did they understand. The sight of it felt like a slap.

'How disgusting! Surely, *kuya*, whoever did this was possessed by a demon!' Said Myla to her elder brother, pressing a towelette to her mouth and nose.

'You should be used to it by now. Seems like it's every month these days there's a corpse dumped on our streets,' replied Butsok. 'The shameless fucks have made our place their trash heap of choice for everyone they chop up.'

The two stepped out from the crowd congregating around the body and walked to the court's exit.

'Why do you think, kuya?' Asked Myla.

'This way it's someone from Dreamland who'll get picked up as the suspect. Another reason so they can erase our place from the map of the city. That simple.'

'But . . . how? We don't even know whoever that man is, and he certainly isn't from here.'

'If the police claim that dead guy is from Dreamland, those of us who live here can't say otherwise.'

'Like that. C'mon, little one, you'll be late.'

The siblings exited the court and got on the line for the tricycle. Butsok waited until Myla got on one.

'Ey you take care,' Butsok bid his sister, then mussed her hair.

'Kuya stop that, my hair!' And playfully slapped away her brother's hand. Butsok laughed.

'Okay okay, just go.' Butsok rapped twice on the tricycle's roof and it zoomed away, out of Dreamland.

'Ey, 'Tsok!' called a voice from behind him. When he looked back it was Jeffrey, he was loafing at Old Lady Aling Mareng's gulaman drink stall. Butsok walked over.

'What's good?' He fist-bumped Jeffrey.

'You saw the corpse at the court, huh?' Jeffrey asked, loading weed into a pipe.

'Ahhhh, yeah. Where'd he come from?' Butsok replied.

'Second one now, 'Tsok,' Jeffrey sniffed and hacked phlegm on to the asphalt.

'As far as I know that's the first one this month.'

'Awww no no, ya dolt. What I meant was that's the second case.'

Butsok's brows creased in thought, he couldn't wrap his head around what Jeffrey was saying. Second case? Jeffrey lit the pipe, coughed from the first hit. Took another drag then passed the pipe to Butsok.

'Brother, the victims are gay guys,' said Jeffrey between coughs. 'First corpse they got from Hagonoy, then that's the second one they found here. Same modus of the killer, how he did them in. Here and in Hagonoy the corpses look like they were killed the same.'

Butsok recalled how the corpse in the court looked. He took a deep lungful from the pipe and was drowned in the minute and a half of silence that came with the ganja hit. When his focus returned, he grasped for an apt reply to Jeffrey's information bomb.

'I wonder what kind of sick trip the killer is on?' Butsok coughed and returned the pipe to Jeffrey, now moist from his own palms.

'Can't say it was a robbery from how his face is all banged up. That's just unnecessary brutality.'

'Two now, you said? And what are the police doing letting the killer get two under his belt?'

'Who the fuck knows, might be it was them all along right?'

'Hmmmm. Wouldn't be surprised. Didn't get out to drive folks today?' Butsok changed the subject.

'I'm all lined up, at least my trike is. Still has a ways to go at the rate things are moving now. Downtime is for lighting up.'

'Ah . . . well, I'll go ahead, ah? Dad is going to work now and nobody will be home,' Butsok fist-bumped a goodbye to Jeffrey.

Jeffrey called after him. 'Ah, where's your mother by the way?'

'Chapel, why?'

'It's nothing, just wanted to offer her some products from the missus. New Avon and other stuff.'

'Just go to the church. She'll be there all day.'

'Thanks, 'Tsok!'

'Alright, see you, ah.'

He walked back to the court and found that the crowd had grown. The funk of the gathered, unwashed bodies had multiplied in proportion, too.

The body at the centre of the circle was like a mound of shit that had attracted buzzing flies to its proximity, until a police siren broke through the noise of the gossiping voices. The crowd thinned out immediately. Particularly quick to exit were people who still had cases to work out with the law and those who couldn't hide their obvious state of drug addiction.

Two mobile cruisers brought to the scene a group of uniformed officers and crime scene investigators. As the group started walking, the crowd continued to thin and break, making a path for them that led straight to the dead man.

'Make this area clear,' declared the eldest officer who wore glasses to his subordinates.

'Yes, sir,' replied the youngest uniformed officer. 'Attention everyone, everyone who can hear, and all you mothers. You all can go home now and see to making your kids breakfast.'

A few people took some paces back while others did as they were bid and exited the scene to return to their hovels. A yellow roll of police tape took the place of the crowd around the body. Cameras clicking and flashing replaced the ambience of voices and grunts. These pictures and the accompanying headlines would later tell how a gay man was found dead on the filthy court of Dreamland, stab wounds all over, with his dick stuffed in his own mouth.

Butsok also stepped away, maintaining a distance from the law and their fussing. He only did so to better observe the whole picture of how they processed the crime scene. The image of the corpse stained his mind. Bloody briefs worn like a hat. A severed penis. From where he stood, Butsok could clearly witness everything, take it all in with amazement and fidelity.

12

What brought Rosa up from kneeling on the pews were two wolf whistles, a much-anticipated sound that brought waves of gladness radiating from her solar plexus, spreading upwards to beat against her chest.

Before she left the chapel she looked back at the crucifix and whispered a relieved, barely heard, 'Oh God, thank you.'

Jeffrey was waiting outside with his tricycle. Absolutely everyone in the hood knew that he hadn't finished paying the monthly instalment for the vehicle. Jeffrey owed a lot to his uncle, a retired soldier

She was excited when she boarded the tricycle and her heart was light as it noisily made its way away from the chapel. They were headed for Barangay Mabini, just a few blocks away from Dreamland, and when they got there Jeffrey parked at the only vulcanizing shop that bordered the Inners. The shop was owned by her mother's ex. They both walked down the narrow alley, making a beeline for Mang Ruben's dirty ice cream shop, a remedy for the stifling heat they felt in both senses.

'Oy, Jepoy! What's good?' Greeted the shirtless, sweaty man mixing the ice cream in a giant steel bowl.

'Can't complain. Got anything free?' Jeffrey asked the man.

'Fifteen minutes, okay, *Poy ah*? Those people inside now are done, give them some time to dress,' replied the man.

'Ah . . . Okay, we'll just wait.'

They both sat on the long bench that sat across the aluminium door. Jeffrey's hand was on Rosa's thigh. Rosa, meantime, had a hanky to her lips, head bowed, and still seemed to be mouthing prayers.

'Rosa, you okay?' Asked Jeffrey, while squeezing her thigh, his enthusiasm apparent and barely contained.

'Of course. What's bothering you?' Said Rosa in a tone that echoed all the other women whose identity had been carved from churches Hail Marys and Our Fathers resonated.

'Ey, you haven't said anything since the chapel. You didn't miss me, ha?' He teased and his fingers danced closer to her inner thigh.

'You know I always look forward to seeing you,' she teased back.

'Hmmm . . . Or likely he got a taste of you last night, which would explain why you aren't excited today?' Jeffrey said.

'I already told you, Delfin and I haven't been doing it for a long time,' Rosa said, acting annoyed.

'Oh, ey, why don't you seem excited to me?' Jeffrey was pushing it.

'Because Butsok has been on my mind, Jeff,' Rosa's eyes started to moisten.

'Why, what's the problem with Butsok?' Jeffrey queried. Rosa was hiccupping her tears and Jeffrey rubbed her back to comfort her.

'Epoy!' The man mixing ice cream cried out, 'You two can go up now.' That got Jeffrey's attention immediately, a sure sign that his brain was still on the sexual congress to come and not because he was really worried about Rosa worrying about Butsok.

He gently pulled Rosa up as she was still wiping her tears. They both traversed the narrow, muddy path that led to the rickety stairway, up to the Wantupayb Room, meaning it cost 125 pesos as the parlance went among the Mabini locals.

Clearly the room was on its knees. The interior looked like it was only one termite signature away from utter collapse, but none of that deterred Jeffrey or diminished his eagerness as he quickly closed the wafery plywood shingle that acted as a door. Rosa was still sobbing, albeit gently. And finally, Jeffrey was forced to take stock and notice that Rosa was gutted. Her sobbing had not ceased or even lessened in strength.

'Well, will you just tell me what the hell is up with Butsok?' He couldn't stop the edge in his tone. Rosa didn't reply but tried to stifle her staccato breathing, calm herself down from her unspooling emotional high. Then she stood and took her top off.

Once again Jeffrey beheld, after countless other occasions, the unfettered sexual faculty of a fifty-year-old fanned to a resurgent peak after that fire had almost died from years without intimacy, without anywhere to direct its formidable craving.

Jeffrey, speechless, like a dog gone mad, directed his hunger and lips to Rosa's chest at the same time stroking her breasts in happy zeal.

13

Delfin and his daughter Myla arrived at their house at the same time. They found Butsok inside cooking tonight's dinner.

'O, why are you cooking here? Your mother not around again?' Mang Delfin queried while taking his shoes off.

Butsok dropped what he was doing and grabbed his father's right hand, putting the back of it to his forehead in a traditional sign of deference to the elderly. 'Might still be at the chapel, Pa.'

'She's making that damn chapel her personal loitering ground. Even worse, she's neglected all the chores at her very own house!' Delfin hurled the shoe he'd just taken off at the wall. Myla immediately picked up the stray footwear and put it on their small rack.

'Might be she was just out late doing some community service.'

'Curse that woman! She'll get back nothing good from—pwe! Would have been better if she'd taken Menchie up on her offer to work at their grocery store and gotten a monthly salary instead of begging from God knows who! Every night it's the same shit,' and Delfin did a beeline for the small room with only a curtain across to cordon it off from the rest of the house.

Butsok turned to his younger sister, 'And how's it been at work, ha?'

'Very tiring, kuya, I really just want to go to bed,' she replied with shoulders sloped, sleepless eyes ringed with dark swaths.

'Ey, then go. Get some rest. I'll set aside food for you, so you'll have something to dig up in case you get hungry later.'

'Rest? Well, I wish. Just you wait until Nanay gets in. We're in for a mess that's for sure.'

Butsok could only scratch the back of his head. Back at the kitchen, he went back to finish cooking. When Mang Delfin came out of the room he held the revolver in his hand like a prized pet. He regarded it like it was the first time he'd held it, stroking it like a puppy or like a Nazarene figure made to be touched by devotees.

'Myla, child!' He called out to his daughter. 'Go see if the jar over there has oil in it.'

'Yes, Pa!' Myla replied.

Myla grabbed the jar beside the yellowing dish rack and, upon touching the glass, was immediately assaulted by extreme worry. And Butsok? He stood around confused and nervous, so jittery that he was unable to help his sibling. Because the jar was empty. No oil.

Myla walked slowly to Mang Delfin, trying to gauge her father's mood.

'Pa?'

'Oy, where's the oil?' Mang Delfin queried.

'Pa, we don't have any oil,' Myla replied, the tone of it was conciliatory, trying to defuse the rising temperature that she knew was almost inevitable.

'Goddamn! I reminded you kids this morning, ah!' he seethed. 'Butsssoooook! Butsooook!'

Butsok hurried to the *sala* to his father, a distance that only took three steps from their tiny kitchen.

'Pa?'

'Didn't I tell you this morning that there needs to be oil in that jar when I come back?' Mang Delfin challenged his son with this unassailable fact.

'But, Pa. Y-you didn't l-leave any money for it. The amount you gave me this morning was only enough for the rice.'

The broken rhythm in Butsok's voice belied his frayed nerves. What his son had just told him made Mang Delfin stop in his tracks and forget his anger for a moment, leaving him searching his faded memory and trying to remember exactly what he'd done that morning. But the look on his face already told Butsok that his father had indeed forgotten the fact that he hadn't given his son anything extra to buy oil.

Butsok's anxiety was so intense he was shivering, looking like someone had upended a bucket of ice on his skinny frame. Myla breathed a sigh of relief. From the corner, the sound of a door opening interrupted the three of them. They all turned their heads, and the siblings watched their mother Rosa sheepishly enter their tiny house. Brother and sister's anxiety shot up again when, looking back to their father, they saw that the lines on his forehead had tripled from what was already a smooth calm just moments previous.

'Takes all morning 'til night, huh? I bet you'll be sainted in no time at all!' Delfin greeted his wife.

Butsok and Myla exchanged nervous glances, like they were trying to draw strength from each other for the upcoming night of a waking nightmare.

'Thing is there were plenty of relief goods to be repacked and shipped to the people in Bulacan who lost their homes to the big fire,' Rosa replied.

'FUCK! What do we care about the idiots in Bulacan? We're minding our own business in Manila and you want to poke your nose into Bulacan? What fuckery is that?' Delfin's tone was raspy and cruel, phlegm making his voice gargly and distorted. Rosa kept quiet. She headed for the bedroom. Delfin only stared daggers at her back while the siblings were frozen in place.

Butsok unfucked himself from indecision and tried to distract the old man, saying softly, 'Pa, let's go and eat, food's cooked.'

In reply Delfin put grips under their small table and flipped it over. Fortunately, Butsok hadn't laid any food on the table yet. Delfin put the revolver in his jeans and strode to the room, to Rosa. Butsok and Myla stayed in the sala, could only refuse to not hear the sounds of the cruel beating taking place a few steps away.

'FUCK YOUR MOTHER! ALL THAT CHURCH TIME AND YOU'RE STILL A BITCH! UGHM!'

'AHHHRGH! WHAT DID I DO TO YOU, DELFIN? UGHMHMF!'

'DIRTY BITCH! YOU PROUD OF THAT ROTTEN PRIEST, HA?'

Myla couldn't help but weep. Butsok put his arms around his sister, unable to deny the fear making his knees shake. All they could do was wait out the storm.

'HUHGHUHUKKH! FOR GOD'S SAKE STOP IT, DELFIN! S-STOP—UGHGH!'

'WHAT YOU REALLY WANT IS TO GET THAT UNRIPE PRIEST TO SCREW YOU SO YOU CAN SAY ALL THAT TIME AT THAT CHAPEL WAS FUCKING QUALITY! YOU SHIT! UGH!'

'YOU'RE HURTING ME, DELFIN! STOP IT!'

'DE-D-DELFIN? NO, NOT THAT! A DEMON MIGHT POSSESS YOU! HAVE MERCY, DELFIN!'

Butsok couldn't stand it any more. He let go of Myla and strode into the room, brushing aside the curtains. His mother was splayed on the floor, sweaty, in tears, and snotty while his father was fiddling with something in the revolver.

'Pa! Please stop this, Pa!' Butsok shouted.

'Get out, you! You don't want any of this!' Delfin raised his hand as if to strike his son.

Butsok was ready to dodge though, fearful as he was, even as his father pushed him out of the room. The next thing Butsok heard was the noise of steel, zings of bullets and empty casings falling to the floor.

'HERE, HERE IS YOUR GOD!'

'GHSHGAHHH!'

'AHHHHGWHSKUPOO!'

And then the siblings heard, not the pop of a gun, but a heavy noise of something wet colliding with a hard object. They were unsure whether to be relieved or further afraid of what they could only surmise was a mystery behind the closed curtain of their parents' room.

'Myla,' Butsok gave his sister the loose change from his shorts. 'Go and buy some oil from Aling Surping's store.' Myla took the coins and made a quick exit, grabbing the jar as she passed the door.

Only a mewling cry could be heard from beyond the curtains, nothing more from the bass voice of their father. The nightmare was quiet for a moment. Butsok, unable to think of anything else to do, went ahead and put their food in serving plates, setting the table, waiting for his mother and father to emerge.

Rosa was the first to come out, just like always. She had her hair up and back, her clothes dishevelled, and fresh blood was flowing down her nose. Butsok went to his mother and embraced her. Patted her on the back.

'Ma, let's sit and eat,' was the only thing Butsok thought to say. Rosa could only sniff and sob.

'BUTSOOOOOAOWKKKK!' shouted Mang Delfin

Butsok seated his mother then fearfully walked to the room. Rosa sat at the dinner table with a thousand-yard stare, remembering what she'd told Jeffrey. A fresh swath of tears rolled down her cheeks, bruised and inflamed from the beating she'd taken.

'Butsok, my son . . .' she murmured to herself, while the blood on her nose dripped to the table, falling in time with the beating of her doomed heart.

14

A humid night, the spirit of that heat in the wind foretold the coming of rain, infusing the souls of those in one corner of the Inners.

Butsok could only hold on to his silence when Marife laid out the situation to him. This only further incensed Marife, since the lack of response from her boyfriend meant that her anger couldn't find any fuel. The normally patient and kind woman found herself full of ire at her guy, with her many questions answered only by a mum Butsok.

'How do you explain this, Butsok?' she said in an interrogatory tone. 'How?'

Butsok's gaze took in the filthy kids playing on the street. No reply. His ears mute, like they had a cordon of silence.

'Butsoook? Answer me, please? Huhhmhuhm . . .' begged Marife, unable to contain the tears.

Butsok took the cigarette stuck on one ear and lit it. In the inhale and exhale that followed, he felt like the smoke shaped the sigh he wanted to express.

Marife suddenly stood and the stool under her toppled over. She grabbed the seated Butsok by the collar and shook. 'Neither of us is an idiot, Butsok!' Butsok dropped the cigarette, ashes scattered everywhere. Not getting the reaction she wanted, Marife shook him harder. No emotion there. Butsok's face remained blank. The street kids continued to play. Butsok hung his head.

'S-Sorry . . .' he stutteringly said.

Marife intensified her shaking and tried mightily to stop the sobbing that threatened to burst out at any second. When she released him, Butsok stood and took a few steps away from the argument.

'That's it, you're just leaving?'

Butsok stopped, inclined his head slightly towards his girlfriend and shook his head. Marife tracked him with her sorrowed gaze as he picked up the cigarette then righted the stool. He sat down and started smoking again.

A beat of silence then the rowdy cries of the street kids playing tag intruded on their spat. Sporadic raindrops started to fall, sounding like hesitant drums on the tin roofs.

'Rain come down! Rain come down!' shouted the frolicking kids.

'We're adults now, Butsok. No longer innocent,' she said. 'Who do you want me to blame this on, ha?'

Butsok's lips stayed silent, only using them to smoke, staring at the kids trying to catch the erratic raindrops on their palms. He was clearly trying not to smile.

And Marife noticed this. She spotted a good-sized rock, said 'You even have the temerity to smile?!' and hurled it at Butsok. Her aim was true. Good effect on Butsok's temple.

'What the fuck? That hurt!' The rock surprised Butsok. Caught off-guard, his verbal ejaculation was high-pitched and made him cradle half his face. Slowly, he peeked at his hand. It was bloody. Feeling across his eyebrow, a lump was already forming. He glared angrily at Marife, who returned his intensity with her own ocular daggers.

'Butsok, my pussy now packs more pus than your dick has semen,' Marife said accusingly and turned away, walking off into the sprawl of alleys.

'Rain come down! Rain come down!' the kids continued to chant.

15

Her name on the violet clearbook was 'Starr' with two Rs. The manager, whose name was 'Cherry Blossom', claimed she was one of those on the menu list that was straight out of the prestigious universities along U-belt—guaranteed young, clean, fresh, and first class.

Starr was one of the so-called Solar Angels. Which meant she was one of those assigned to the kind of patrons whose willies were hungry first thing in the morning. They craved a different kind of meal, these Johns who broke their fast on sating their lust. Most days, their customers were white junkies who couldn't sleep and only the Solar Angels' ministrations could knock them off to their dreams; sometimes BPO overlords whose only free time to party was during daylight hours; and then there's the office boys for whom 'lunch-out' meant eating black noodles.

One morning, Starr found two guys waiting for her at the club. One was a slant-eyed Japanese and the other a Filipino with distinctly Indian features. Cherry greeted Starr with two air kisses on her cheeks.

'You're a bit late,' Cherry said in a tone that was half-query and half-worry, with a grin forming on her mouth. 'That guy's hanging around waiting for you.'

'Thing is, my brother's been insisting he drop me off here. And you know that's not an ideal situation, right?' Starr said in a tone that wasn't kidding around.

'Let's not make him wait around again, they've been long-time loyal customers, you know,' Cherry retorted with brows rising and falling.

'Should have made him just choose from the menu,' Starr said, applying glitzier make-up over her pale foundation.

'Ditz! You're obviously the one he comes back for,' Cherry teased, pinching Starr in her side. Starr jumped from the surprise.

'So now we know better than the client?'

Starr continued to apply her work make-up, finishing with a flourish of lipstick.

'You know, I asked him nicely to wait. Don't be picky, girl, it's all cash in the end,' added Cherry, her exquisitely shaped left eyebrow rising.

'That so? Well, thanks, ha?' Starr dumped her make-up into her bag and turned her back so quickly her hair swished like a whip. Cherry was left staring at her fading back with one eyebrow frozen high. Starr approached the two guys seated on the club's enormous couch.

'Hi there Atsuo, good morning! How are you?' Starr greeted the slant-eyed guy with a happy tone in her best English. The man stood up and embraced her with the intent to grope. His hands went down to fondle her thighs. She didn't pay it any mind.

'Am kood, am kood!' The slant-eyed man said, nodding his head.

'Who is he?' Starr indicated the other man beside Atsuo by pouting her lips in his direction.

'Ahhh! Renato-san, my, uh, doraibaa, yes! Doraibaa! Yes, yes!' Quickly replied chinky eyes.

The Indian-looking local held out his hand for her to shake and said in the local vernacular, 'Good morning, I am Renato ma'am. I'm the driver for Mr Atsuo.'

'Okay, hi Renato!' Starr greeted him.

'Oke, oke. Shar wi ko now?' Said chinky eyes.

'Let's go!' Starr seconded and put her arm around his. They both walked out of the club with Renato trailing.

Cherry was near the entrance, postured as if waiting for someone. Atsuo brought out his wallet, bursting to the brim with bills and put a wad between Cherry's ample cleavage. Cheery whispered something to Atsuo that made the guy nod and grin. Starr couldn't hear the exchange and waved it off as inconsequential.

'Huait phor me in frownt, Starr,' said Atsuo. Starr did as requested, and walked to the front of the club as Renato ran down to the basement parking. A few moments later a white Honda Civic emerged and stopped right in front of Starr. Renato came down and opened the passenger door for her, while Atsuo was still talking to Cherry.

'Been driving for Atsuo long?' She asked the driver in Tagalog while they waited.

'Ah . . . Almost six months now, ma'am.'

'Ah . . . This car seems new?' Starr asked. 'We just rode taxis before this.'

'Pretty new, ma'am,' Renato replied.

The passenger door opened and Atsuo got in. 'Res ko, Rekanto!' Atuso told the driver.

Atsuo's right hand went to Starr's neck and down to her chest, then back up to her lips, while his left hand fondled her smooth thigh. Starr took all of it in stride. Her gaze would drift to the rearview mirror every so often, waiting for the inevitable peek from the driver.

She met every thump in her chest, confronting her nerves head on.

16

'Being a mortician is more complex than studying algebra.'

This is the mantra that Mang Delfin had drilled into Butsok from a young age. For his part, the young man did not have an opinion about it at all, since algebra held zero interest for him from the time when he was still in school, up to when he dropped out. Only selling ice-buko, the frozen sweet made from coconut, concerned him after school didn't work out.

Whenever Kris, the embalming assistant, wasn't around, Mang Delfin would bring over Butsok to the morgue. Menandro Mortuary Services was a 16-peso tricycle trip from Dreamland. At the tender age of six, Butsok was already a common sight at Menandro's, since his father had been working there for nigh a decade. The cold room with the fishy, acrid smells wasn't anything new to him, nor were the rows of corpses covered in their white lab shrouds.

It was midnight when, one day, Mang Delfin woke up Butsok and told him they needed to go to Menandro's. Apparently, they really needed to go. SPO3 Malonzo, a neighbourhood police officer, was asking a favor from Alvin Tisu, Mang Delfin's boss and the owner of the mortuary. There was nary a favor that Menandro's said no to when it came to Malonzo the cop. Aside from bringing steady business of bodies to the morgue, there were other enterprises that their Chinese boss was involved in with the police officer. Matters of trade with the law could only encompass protection while other systems higher than those were the same ones that brought in the unlucky to the very same morgue.

‘’Tsok! ’Tsok!’ His father incessantly tapped his shoulder.

Butsok wiped his face as he opened his eyes and regarded his father, a blurry image in front of him.

‘Po? Taoahhhhhhaaywr? Da-Dad?’ He said yawning as he searched his head for words to answer his father.

‘Get up now, you. Boss called and we need to be there now,’ Mang Delfin said. Butsok made half his body rise from the couch that was his bed, stretched his weary bones. After a few moments of just staring at nothing, he stood and went to the sink. Splashing water on his face helped to dispel the sleep and clue him in with what was happening.

‘Dad, how many are we going to work on?’ Butsok asked as he dressed.

‘Just one,’ Mang Delfin replied, packing his bag.

‘One? Ey, there’s a twenty-four-hours mortuary near Mabini, right?’ Inquired Butsok.

Mang Delfin stopped his packing and shouted back, ‘Stop your yapping and get your ass moving, you lazy fuck.’

Butsok could only shut up and finish dressing up. ‘Let’s go, kid,’ Mang Delfin urged and they both left the house in the still hours.

***

At the mortuary there were three police officers waiting at the lobby inside. SPO3 Malonzo was dressed in civvies, a big guy in a leather jacket and acid-washed jeans. The other two were cops in uniform. This meant that their boss, Alvin Tsiu, had already been there and had opened the place for these three, his *friends* in the force.

'Good evening to you, chief!' Mang Delfin greeted SPO3 Malonzo.

'Good morning now.'

'Ay! Good morning, yes, since it's past midnight now, chief!' Mang Delfin corrected himself. He then turned to the other two cops and greeted them with the same chirpy tone.

'You know what to do here, right? We've talked, your boss and I,' SPO3 Malonzo told Mang Delfin.

'Okay po, okay po!' Mang Delfin quickly replied.

'Who's this with you?' Inquired the cop in charge, pointing his lips at Butsok.

'Ah . . . That's my eldest son, chief!' Delfin grinned.

'Good morning, sirs,' Butsok said but nobody acknowledged him.

'All right all right, you're both good to carry on,' Malonzo added, waving his hand to dismiss them as he turned to the exit and walked out of the mortuary. His two shadows, the uniformed cops, trailed behind and then only the father and son were left.

When Mang Delfin heard the satisfying sound of the mobile car's motor hacking and rumbling to a start, he immediately locked the door to the embalming room. It was the sound he'd been waiting for, so they could begin. Father and son donned surgical masks and gloves.

''Tsok, would you open that bag,' Mang Delfin pointed his son to the body bag the three cops had left as he laid out the tools of his trade—the mortician's best friends—on a tray.

Butsok slowly unzipped the body bag. When it opened, Butsok beheld a man with an amputated penis in his mouth. Unzipping the bag further revealed that the corpse's arms had wounds, marks, and bruises from strong blows. They were all fairly fresh.

Reaching the torso, the unzipped body bag revealed the man's intestines were peeking out of his stomach. Dozens of stab wounds and slices were the cause of this mess. Butsok couldn't help but shake his head at the poor state of the corpse.

'You might forget to list it all down again. Don't go off half-cocked and reckless,' reminded Mang Delfin.

'Yes, father,' Butsok nodded and went to the supply cabinet, bringing out a tickler notebook and ballpen before going back to the mauled corpse's side.

Butsok started to list down and count the wounds and the other violent indignities that marked the poor corpse. As Butsok undressed him, he also wrote down anything found on the man.

What came to mind was Jeffrey's story. He recalled the corpse at the court and now the one in front of him. He continued to be mystified.

17

Butsok emerged from the room limping. He made a beeline for the kitchen where his mother was, again, inconsolably crying. Butsok put a hand to her back and comforted her. The wall clock said it was 12.58 in the early morning.

'Didn't Myla even send a text message, mother?' Butsok asked her. She only shook her head.

A beat and then a longer beat stretched out between them. He made his mother coffee, yet still she said nothing. He knew there were more bruises than just the visible ones on her arms and face. Like many cases of violence at home, the longer the beatings went on, the more normal they seemed, moving into daily life like a piece of furniture or just another chore. Often, this made it easier to let it happen.

'Myla's cell phone isn't even on, I called her earlier. Now it's past 1 a.m., mom,' worry thickened Butsok's voice.

Mang Delfin came out of the room, scratching his pot belly. He walked to the kitchen sink to get a drink. Butsok was silent while his mother played it off like Delfin wasn't even there.

'Oy, why don't you both go to sleep?' Mang Delfin asked.

'Myla's still not home, dad.'

'Ey, what are you still doing here then? Why don't you go fetch her?'

'But I don't even know where she is,' Butsok scratched his head.

'Ey, aren't you the one who drops her off at work?'

'Opo.'

'And you don't know because?'

'I only take her to the tricycle terminal.'

'You all know you're crazy. Your sister herself tells me you're the one who drops her off at work. And when I text her that I'll be the one to take her home, she says you'll be the one to fetch her from work. So, what in all fuck is the truth here?'

'Really don't know dad, all I know is the tricycle station is where I leave her.'

'Insane, all of you!' Said Mang Delfin as he stomped his way back to the bedroom. He came out again minutes later, already dressed, the unmistakable lump of the revolver on his side, under the shirt.

'You, Rosa. You're just going to sulk and be dramatic on the table I see,' Mang Delfin put his pointer finger against his wife's temple, digging the nail into her skin. 'Your girl, your daughter, has not come home at all and yet it's like it's just nothing to you, you pathetic bitch.'

'Dad, please stop it,' Butsok interrupted.

'You want a taste, huh?' Mang Delfin halfway raised his arm as if to level a blow at his son.

'You're the one who's pathetic.'

Mang Delfin—and Butsok, who couldn't help but cringe at the blow he thought was incoming—both stopped in their tracks.

'Whore, what did you just say?'

'You're the most pathetic thing here, is what I said,' said Rosa, holding back a sob.

'Mother . . .' Butsok tried to placate her, worrying that she'd get another beating for her boldness to speak back.

'Me? I'm pathetic?' Mang Delfin repeated. 'Pathetic is what I am, huh?' He enunciated the words in rough staccato and in a tone of threat.

'You deaf shit! You really want me to repeat—'

BLAG!

Rosa fell from the chair and her chin thumped on the table. She lay sprawled on the floor, either side of her lips lined with blood.

'I'm pathetic! Right?!' Mang Delfin opened his eyes wide at her, challenging her to say it again.

Butsok inserted himself between his parents. Rosa hugged her son's leg, shaking and crying. In her thumping heart, worry and loathing tried to outrace each other.

'Dad, please stop it, stop it!' Butsok waved his arms in front of him, pre-emptively warding off the blows he knew were coming.

'Hoy, Rosa! Is that what you've been learning in church all these years, you bitch of a whore?' Mang Delfin still had his hand raised, ready to strike.

'Dad, please, let's just go find Myla,' Butsok pleaded.

'You're all fucking insane!' Mang Delfin cried out then swiped the coffee cup from the table with a backhand. The coffee spilled on Butsok.

'OW! That's damn hot!' Butsok screamed and fanned his shirt. He was blowing on the part of his arm that had been doused with coffee, as if the pitiful wind could alleviate the burn.

The cup broke near Rosa's feet.

'We still need to find your sister so get moving now!' Mang Delfin said and turned his back on them, walking to the kitchen.

With both arms, Rosa was still mightily clinging to Butsok's leg.

Rosa sobbed her next words out. 'N-no need t-to find huh-her, s-son,' she said as she fell into a deep sobbing when a trickle of blood mixed with a rivulet of oil trickled from the inside of Butsok's thigh. It dropped onto Rosa's hands. Butsok hurriedly wiped this hot mix of blood and oil on the hem of his shirt, still wanting to hide it.

'BUTSOK! YOU COMING BOY?' Mang Delfin shouted.

'Give me a moment, please,' Butsok replied.

Rosa still refused to let Butsok's leg go.

'Mom, we've got to go out and search for Myla,' Butsok said, peeling his mother's arms off as gingerly as he could muster. 'That's it, c'mon, open your hands please. We'll both be getting it bad at this rate.'

Yet Rosa, after relaxing her arms for a moment, only hugged Butsok even tighter. This went on for a few minutes until Mang Delfin returned from waiting in the kitchen.

'SONOVA, WHAT THE FUCK IS—'

'DELFIN, YOU SON OF A WHORE! YOU DEMON!' Rosa snatched the curse right out of her husband's mouth. Startled at his mother's return to boldness, Butsok raised his guard again.

'Ah? Really want to try my patience, ha?' Mang Delfin unholstered the revolver from his side and pointed it at his wife.

'MYLA IS IN THE HOSPITAL, YOU SON OF A BITCH! SHE'S NEVER GOING TO WALK AGAIN!' Rosa screamed at Mang Delfin.

Father and son froze in their movement. For a few seconds only the insects and the machine hum of the electric fan made a sound.

'What the fuck are you saying, ha woman?' Mang Delfin asked, slowly lowering the gun.

'Mom?' Butsok seconded the question.

Rosa's heart was still thumping wildly, and her soul felt like it was being separated from her body. 'Your daughter is never going to walk again, Delfin!'

This kind of information needed time to sink into the skulls of pitiable men. Like a frayed thread trying to be inserted into the eye of a needle, or a huge fist thrust into the ass of a newbie prison inmate, neither father nor son could wrap his head around Rosa's declaration.

'When I came home earlier, I was calling for you, I was begging you, Delfin!' Rosa's voice was thick with emotion. 'Yet you were too busy with whatever stupid shit you were doing!'

She continued her tirade. 'I told you to listen to me, even for a moment, but no! What did you do? You smashed me around the house because there was no oil for your stupid gun! You even wanted me to buy it for you! Remember now?'

Mang Delfin's mouth opened and closed in silence, desperately trying to latch on to a retort. Butsok was still in deep shock, unable to believe what his mother had said at all. Again, a thin rivulet of oil and blood made its way down his pant leg. He didn't even bother wiping it away.

18

He was running. Running as fast as he could with the agile feet of an eight-year-old. He was chasing after his own youth in the empty lots, alleys, basketball courts, and streets. On his toasted skin was the scorching heat of the season. Inhaling the dust. Competing with his friends on who had more welts and dirt-lines on the skin. Bottling up the rising blubbery when teased. Laughing at himself when he tripped. The sun setting on his fury.

When he did wake up, in the wisdom and maturity of a nine-year-old, the confusion had still not departed. The inside of his skull was wrapped with fright and anxiety with the curtains that now signalled his twilight hours instead of the clouds in the heavens.

Marife's waifish body was gyrating above him, pounding against his groin, her contrastingly bountiful chest would angle away from the powerful thrusts and sway of her hips. While Marife was giving it her all in an intense routine worthy of a porn star, you couldn't see a trace of passion from the one seated beneath her. Slowly, this state of dispassionate coolness dawned on Marife.

'You about done?' Marife asked while doing her best to continue her dance.

'Nooo n-not yet, d-don't stooop. Let's get there together, ahhh . . .' said the one beneath like he was ticking off a list. Marife was a professional and she continued to do the professional thing, which was to see this all through despite the inevitable fading within three minutes that had become more and more common. What she hated most was needing to fake the end.

'Ahhhh . . . ahhh? Uhhhhhh!'

If the ceiling of the room they were in could only list the kind of worry Butsok had by letting him stare at it in moments like these, then the whole area would be full by now. His mind raced through so many what-ifs and living nightmares.

'Ahhhh! Fuuuuck!'

'Ahhhhhhhhrgh!'

When his mother peeked through the curtains, she could do nothing but stare in shock and shed a tear at the vulgar sight.

'You shameless devil!' She screamed so intensely that it came out in a gargle.

From that day on, those lips never curled into a smile again. Neither could she ever draw the curtains open again without being cautious since the consequence was wounds and bruises on her face.

'Ohmahgod! Ohhhh!'

On Valentine's they'd eat at Jollibee and head straight for a subdivision in Hagonoy, Taguig—a vast area that was still being developed. An empty place, devoid of community and thus lightless and mostly kept unlit. Except for sporadic light posts, it was easy to lose to the night here and so it was also easy to find a dark corner among the tall grass, and there, give in eagerly to the call of their bodies.

His cell phone kept vibrating yet the good vibrations he was feeling were louder, his groans like a dog deprived of his bone. Twelve missed calls he'd find out afterwards, all from Myla. It was dusk when he finally checked. His mother kept screaming, calling for his father, yet the man was still way too concerned with his gun cleaning to even respond. His father told mother to go and buy a refill of oil, to remedy the sorry state of the jar.

* * *

And he'd wake up sweating like a pig, heart racing, throat dry, and eyes in tears. Going back to sleep seemed like a bad choice. He realized that as time went by, there really ought to be an index of improvement in resilience against calamity, seeing as how things tended to go haywire again and again, just like that. A stronger appetite for overcoming adversity was necessary, damn it, if waking nightmares were more dreadful than the ones you had when you slept.

In a corner of his brain his girlfriend Marife was still berating him. Another corner was drowned in his mother's tears. Yet another corner was drenched in the blood of Edmon, whom he abhorred and another man whose name he never got to know.

Far on the horizon came the cries of his younger sister Myla, who had been mauled and crippled by an unknown bastard. He considered all these the ghosts of a ruined youth.

He closed his eyes. Observed the vast dark behind his lids. Many were the voices that echoed in his ears.

They were deafening. He'd open his eyes once again. Rise and head for the kitchen. Down a glass of water. Light a cigarette leaning by the doorway and wish his memories were as impermanent as smoke. In all this it dawned on him that he was more like the cigarette slowly turning to ash—those memories were consuming his very soul into oblivion.

19

With the passing of days, weeks, and months also withered the hopes of Butsok's family to get any kind of justice for Myla and what providence had dealt her.

There was no news of anything happening in the case almost five months on, never mind the investigation that had supposedly been conducted. It was still an open case, yet the family had no idea if the authorities were even trying to look for suspects or they'd consigned the search to the cobwebs.

Aling Rosa's enthusiasm to follow-up on her daughter's case at the precinct never faltered, even if the investigators and the case handlers were equally as enthusiastic on ignoring her pleas or making excuses for their excuses. Their stony faces competed with their creativity. Rosa knew full well the police had zero respect for the people living in their district, and most likely, their fervent hope was that they all simply be erased from the face of Metro Manila.

It was raining in the ungodly early morning hours when Rosa came home one time from what had become her hours of nuisance loitering at the precinct. Delfin was absent. Butsok was getting dressed to go out.

'Nanay, you're soaked! Didn't you see how heavy it's coming down?' Butsok said.

'I was already walking you see, so I said might as well go on home,' she replied and expelled some coughs.

'Any news, then?'

'Ay, they had this awarding event today at their office. They wanted me to come back tomorrow. Oh, but that would be in a few hours, I guess.'

'Awarding, mom? You come in past midnight and soaking wet, did you stick around to watch the awards? Did you celebrate with them at the afterparty?' Butsok made sure to ham up the sarcasm.

'Well, you see, the thing is one of them told me to wait. Said they'd call me. And I did wait. Eh, turns out two officers were getting awards for rescuing a Fil-Chinese businessman from getting kidnapped.'

Butsok froze in front of the filthy mirror in the act of tamping down his hair. He realized how much his mom was sacrificing and the kind of fuckery the police was returning for such efforts at justice, making it look like they were the ones being given the aggravation.

'Those jackasses! They know full well it was a chink-eye that did it to my sister. They sure do well when it comes to the other races, especially when there's a fucking award in it for them. But when it comes to us, the walking starved, not even a finger gets lifted?' Butsok's voice had unconsciously raised in volume.

Aling Rosa had no reply for her son. The fists of Butsok clenched and the veins on his temples stood out, throbbing. While the lines on his forehead and between his eyebrows expressed disgust, he saw the image of his own feelings reflected in the dusty mirror, a powerful thirst for revenge that nevertheless lacked any strength or power.

'Award . . . award . . . Sons of whores! Ey, that's their job, those motherfuckers. With how little the people trust those idiots to do their job, when they actually do something, they get a goddamn award for just doing what we're paying them for!' Butsok punched the wall, cobwebs and dust came down from the ceiling. The mirror moved and settled at an askew angle.

'Son, enough please. I guess that's just how it is. God has his reasons. I'm sure we'll get past this and son, this is always in my prayers,' Aling Rosa said, like it was a declamation she'd memorized. After a beat, she changed the subject, 'But where are you going this late in the night?'

'Going to Menandro . . .' Butsok said.

'Your father's working?'

'Yes, mom. Ikyo came to meet me halfway, over at the billiards on the curb and he said Tatay had left a message with him that I should follow.'

'And your sister?'

'Asleep, for a while now.'

'I meant, how is Myla?'

'No change from when we took her home from the hospital.'

'Oh, I know all that, son. What I really want to know is if she's told you anything at all?'

'Mom, how can someone who hasn't spoken a word for five months and has been staring at nothing, suddenly tell me anything?'

Another long beat. Butsok turned away. 'Going, mom. Just take a bath before you turn in, so you don't get a fever.'

'Be safe out there, son.'

'I will, thanks.'

* * *

As Butsok strolled down the street, he ignited a cigarette, relishing every exhale of smoke. A sudden memory washed over him and made him smile, as if the tumultuous explosion of emotions earlier when he was talking to his mother, had been gently whisked away by the breeze.

'You motherfuckers, you're all motherfuckers,' he whispered to himself.

He hailed a tricycle and got on. Because the streets were empty, he arrived at Menandro in no time. When he got off, he loitered for a bit across the street from the funeral parlour. His waiting was rewarded when some men emerged from the door, he didn't know them but suspected they were police. They all got into a red car and Butsok let it drive some ways down the street before he crossed and went into Menandro. His heart was beating loudly in his chest.

Once inside the processing room, he saw that his father hadn't started yet. Mang Delfin was still laying out his gear. Butsok's anxiety went down a notch.

'You sure took your time,' said Mang Delfin.

'Ah . . . Sorry about that, dad. Ikyo didn't get to me in time.'

'I told that Ikyo to meet you on the road. Eh, how's he going to do that when it's already past midnight and you're nowhere to be found? Where've you been anyway?'

'At Baldo's, dad. He had a racket needed doing, I just helped out some.'

'What racket?'

'Peeling off cables for copper.'

'How much you get?'

'Already gave it to mother.'

'Ah, your mother? Didn't know she was already home. Both of you, I have no idea how to get hold of you, but anyway what did she say about her day?'

'Same. Nothing's changed, dad.'

'Those motherfuckers only know how to get our hopes up. And how to suck up to their bosses. Wastes of goddamn space.'

'Eh, dad, don't you know someone at the precinct?'

'So what if I do?'

'I don't know, maybe you can ask them for help.'

'No way. If I ask them for a favour it's no doubt I won't be able to say no when they ask for one back. Specially with the kind of favours I know they'll want from me,' said Mang Delfin.

Butsok was taken aback, his feelings for his father warring with each other and mixing. His father, the father of his sister who had been brutalized and crippled by some bastard, didn't want to ask a favour from the policemen he knew, for fear of being unable to hold up his end if they did come to call.

'I'll open the bag and start the list,' Butsok said.

He walked to the body bag, donned gloves and a facemask, and slowly pulled down the zipper. Once revealed, Butsok instantly recognized the corpse. He stared at it for a bit until his father quipped.

'That's your friend, eh?' Mang Delfin confirmed.

Butsok wanted to answer but could only stare at his friend's face. It seemed as if he was in a staring contest against the wide-eyed corpse.

'Tsk! This, this is B-Buldan, dad! He lives somewhere in the middle. But what did they s-say happened to him?'

'They said that moron downed some silverware cleaner.'

'Who did?'

'The police. They brought him over. Isn't he your friend?'

'Just on greeting terms.'

'A greeting acquaintance? Come now, I saw you drinking with him at Nestor's.'

'We all drink in everyone else's house around here.'

'Ay, 'Tsok. I'm telling you now, stay away from those gutter rats. He was likely on something, you know. He cut off his wee-wee before he drank the poison,' Mang Delfin shook his head in disbelief.

Butsok pulled the zipper down all the way to Buldan's feet. Regarded the whole body. Saw that the penis had indeed been cut off.

'Where'd they put it, his cock?'

'They didn't find out, said he likely fed it to a dog. But that's what drugs do, you know.'

Butsok started to write on his tickler notebook, slowly at first, turning his back to his father. His wide grin might be hidden by the medical mask, yet his eyes might easily reveal the elation he was trying to keep in check. His father's yapping simply faded into the background.

20

The unit was named Task Force Pebrero and the team had been assigned to investigate and hunt down what was being called the Gay Serial Killer currently roaming Metro Manila. So-called because it was in the month of February when two *identical* murders were ascertained to have the same modus.

The first one was found in Lower Bicutan, Hagonoy—victim was naked, briefs stained with blood and wrapped around the head, body riddled with stab wounds, and his amputated penis stuffed into his mouth. The second one was in Dreamland, the body dumped on the basketball court with the same markings and ill-treatment.

In the investigation that followed, two facts connected the victims: they were both gay, they both frequented Nakpil—a haven for gay streetwalkers. The police still did not have anything on the suspect besides speculation that he was an adolescent male call boy. This was as far as police intelligence had gotten in profiling the so-called 'Gay Serial Killer'.

News of the killer naturally became the talk of the neighbourhood in the Inners, where homosexual addicts and pushers ran rampant. As a corollary, the uncles and fathers who wanted their gay sons to turn away from their sins, the same ones who wanted to pray the gay away, used the killer as a threat and the victims as a cautionary tale.

It had its intended effect on the target demographic. The young gay boys went home earlier, reducing their loitering on the streets, and heading home before full dark. Those still in the closet thought twice about coming out to their friends and family. Business for the blowjob-for-meth gay crew ground to a halt, and overall, a sizeable chunk of the population had been frightened and cowed and became the butt of even more insults.

Butsok was on his way home one time at midnight, and it was as if the streets had been mopped clean. He ran into Emerson, a childhood friend, someone he knew had become secretly highly anxious because of the Gay Serial Killer.

'How's it going, 'Tsok?'

'I'm pretty okay. You?' Butsok shrugged.

'Didn't catch where you were headed?'

'Home. You, too?'

'Ah . . . Same. I'll walk with you.'

Butsok looked back like he was trying to get a sight on something which made Emerson look in the same direction.

''Son, eh, don't you live near the entrance?' Butsok tried to confirm, yet as he was saying that he realized his childhood friend just wanted to walk with him despite their homes being at opposite ends of Dreamland.

No answer from Emerson, whose face was a nervous wreck. Butsok scratched his head. 'Want one?' Butsok held out a Fortune cigarette. Emerson accepted, and Butsok lit it up for his friend, then lit his own afterwards.

'Where did you say you were now, 'Tsok?' Emerson asked.

'Still at my parents.'

'Ah naw, I meant . . . where do you work now?'

'Eh, I don't have a permanent gig these days. I just help my father, at Menandro.'

'Ah . . . Me, I work at Andok's Chicken over at the terminal.'

'Yeah, good gig,' Butsok pointed out with zero interest in his tone. He hadn't asked, so he didn't really give a fuck.

'Ever embalmed anyone famous?'

'Nope. The popular people of course get embalmed at the big mortuaries. Menandro's is pretty small time, you know.'

'Ah . . . Must get plenty of criminals, though?'

'Plenty.'

'Oh yeah, forgot to ask if you guys have relatives in Malate?'

'Don't think so. Why?'

'Eh, one night I, you see, I spotted Mang Delfin. When I greeted him, he said he had just visited one of your uncles there.'

'Ah . . . Could be we do have a relative there that I just didn't know about.'

'Could be . . .'

'Hey, you know 'Son, the serial killer only targets gays right?' Butsok pointed out out of nowhere.

'Yeah, I know. Why bring that up?'

'What do you mean "Why"? I should be asking you that, since you're leaking nervousness out your pores. You live way over there and you're walking with me to my house, which you know full well is way back over at the other end.'

'Excuse me for greeting you and walking with you. That a crime now?' Emerson said defensively.

'Nah.'

'There you go. I'm just trying to catch up, that's all.'

'Just don't go on pretending now,' Butsok spat out.

'Meaning what?'

'Look here, 'Son. I'm turning over here now, right here. Okay? With whatever it is you're doing it's fucking obvious you've just gotten farther away from your house.'

'Fine, be like that. Just wanted to catch up, ah,' Emerson stopped while Butsok turned left into an alley.

'Yeah, go on, you be safe now!' Butsok looked back and waved.

When he'd gone some ways into the deep shadows of the narrow alley, Butsok dove for cover and looked back from his hiding place. His childhood friend had turned back in the direction of his house and scampered. Emerson was running like hell on stealthy feet as if he was some thief casing a joint and Butsok couldn't help but laugh to himself as he emerged from behind some trash cans.

Times like these, he thought chidingly, it paid to be a mortician at a small-time embalming house. One owned by a Chinese merchant suckling on the cocks of the police force.

III

The Machines That Grind Our Guts

21

It felt like the wind might sweep me away any time, my common sense along with it. Thoughts like loitering butterflies flitted around my brain, their flight centred round the recent flurry of events.

Just like the bedbugs on my seat, my sanity was being gnawed away by little mouths and both my ears were ringing; the groan of an old wall fan to my right ear and on my left the alternating staccato of a typewriter and the asthmatic, fetid breathing of the investigator. Couldn't understand shit, me. All I had was nodding and shaking my head at his repeating questions. Questions he would himself answer anyway, since anything I said was used against me and assumed as lies as soon as I spoke them.

The investigators were only looking at one angle—Buldan and I were in cahoots in the robbery, rape, and murder of Che. Said they found a necklace of hers at scene of the crime where Buldan's body had been found. One officer had picked it up near Buldan's head.

This necklace, the report said, was something Che was wearing on the night her murder had taken place. And why would Buldan cut off his dick before he gulped down silverware cleaner? Why, they had an answer for that too. This was proof, the police investigator declared, not only of Buldan's complicity but also tantamount to an admission of guilt for Che's slay-rape-robbery.

Meantime, here's me being a hardass about my crime while my co-conspirator had all but closed the case for them. Woooweee, aren't they so clever? Mental note: Never forget they're pigs.

In my head the story was quite different. I know they knew all about what Buldan and I had talked about when he visited me in jail. I was pretty stupid for letting my guard down. I should always assume that they already knew it all. For my carelessness in forgetting they weren't human but rather police scum, here I was, only just realizing like a fool that even before we'd arrived at the room where Buldan and I lived, all the evidence had already been planted, all potential allegations to fit their story already ironed.

Now that Buldan was dead, I was the only piece of the puzzle left that they needed to complete this appalling picture, this farce orchestrated by Elmer.

'How'd the necklace end up at your rental?' Asked the investigator again, probably for the sixth time.

'Chief, I have no idea po.'

'Apparently it was owned by the victim.'

And for the sixth time I nodded my head at this query.

'You and your friends addicts?'

'Of what, sir?'

With his left hand he slapped a piece of paper on his desk, while his right knocked a mug against my cheek. That's some tough porcelain. I fell from my chair and felt the almost instantaneous bruising where the mug had hit. My saliva on the floor was mixed with a trickle of blood.

'Sit the fuck back down and think about your answers. Clear?' The investigator said, looking down on me. I held my rapidly swelling cheek as I got up and, putting the chair right side up, sat back down.

'Again, you and your friends use drugs?' He asked, fingers floating above the typewriter.

I had no idea what this pig was typing as nothing but lies were being formed from our conversation. I shook my head.

'No?' He clarified.

'N-no, chief,' I shook my head.

If looks could kill, my face wouldn't just be swollen now but riddled with stab wounds. He was cursing and shaking his head. He angrily started typing like the thing had robbed him, robbed his family, of something precious.

'So, who raped the victim first?' He suddenly blurted out.

I must confess I felt a stirring of defiance in my blood at this. Despite my black and blue state, in no shape to fight, I still valiantly battled my reddening vision and my rapidly declining composure.

'The way you ask me it's as if everything's already been proven,' I suddenly said, the words surprisingly tumbling out my mouth. I had quite forgotten again who I was talking to.

With the TAK-TAK of the typewriter silenced the groan of the wall fan rose above the murmuring din of the station. Whatever the fraying of nerves sounded like, that was what I heard as he stood, went over to his leather jacket hanging nearby, and fished out a case of Marlboro reds.

He put one to his lips and lit it. Then he approached the desk, prodded me to take one from the case. My anxiety dipped, I relaxed a bit. I fished a cigarette out. He lit it when I put it to my lips.

'Thanks, chief,' I said sheepishly.

'Welcome.'

I then found myself kissing the cold, filthy floor, beside the chair that had again been upturned from my being clobbered. My nose was against his shoe. Closing my eyes as my senses spun like a prize wheel, I felt the cool concrete of the ground against my chest, the pain in my jaw lulling me into blackness.

22

11 p.m., and as he was walking the streets of Malate, his thoughts wandered to how Edmon—with how many homosexual men called this district home—had been the chosen victim of who was being called the Gay Serial Killer. The guy he knew was kind. Didn't dress like a screaming fag at all. So, the reason for the killer picking Edmon escaped him. Some bouncers in the district could have learned a thing or two about macho carriage and bearing from Edmon.

He finally got to the bar where Edmon had been employed when he was still among the quick. A sorry sight greeted him, the frowns on the employees loitering outside to draw business in were all but inviting, faces drained of all carnality.

Two possible reasons. Edmon's death was still fresh on everyone's minds and actively keeping the johns away. Second, the horrible way that Edmon died weighed on their hearts. Yeah, that only came in second; how he'd been maimed. Like Edmon said when he was still alive, 'Nobody really gives a fuck.' That truth was etched on the faces of the bar boys now, a few weeks after Edmon's corpse was found in Taguig.

Once he stepped inside, he almost did a double take. When he came here last, or for that matter whenever he was actually here, the bar was so full to bursting that he had a hard time even getting beyond the doors. Now it seemed like a sorry excuse for a cemetery, the graves long forgotten and unvisited, not a lit candle among them.

Truth is, he was just waiting for someone to approach. For any soul to offer their condolences to him and console him after the awful news. The news, now weeks old, still festered like an open wound in his heart. He yearned to talk to someone about their shared memory of Edmon.

Unlike when Edmon was still alive, tonight, he only ordered beer out of habit, not to get drunk. The nights here could be endless. This place could be empty of solace. And one forlorn moment could easily stretch into bitterness without hope of sweet release. All your troubles could be raised to the gods of alcohol, nicotine, but only a final alleviation lay in the powers contained within the four walls of a quickie motel.

Quickly emptied three bottles of pale Pilsens. Still no lost soul came to his consolation. Previous friends now looked to be strangers—not even sparing him a merciful glance of interest. Edmon was right: Nobody gave a flying fuck, not really. Everyday violence had numbed everyone into callous bastards.

He paid the bill and walked out. As he stood on the curb in front of the bar, regarding the loitering men who were begging for business with their eyes, he never said a word. Only the cigarette smoke and blinking neon lights spoke. Only the voice of the balut vendor cried out in the sprawling, audient void of the city.

House lizards were louder in their syncopated yawps, and he could feel the whispers and stares following him as he walked away from the bar.

Memories of Edmon played through his head the further away he walked, heading out of the district into Greater Manila. Images of delightful recklessness and frustration, of freedom through song, dance, and love. He barely noticed the tears that fell down his cheeks.

'Mang Delfin!' Someone called out to him. He froze in his tracks and his wandering brain snapped back to the moment. Hurrying to wipe the tears, he tried his best to regain his composure.

Whoever had called him was surely from his *barangay*, one of his neighbours, as they'd called him Mang Delfin. Not Adolf, as he was known on these streets.

'Mang Delfin, where'd you come from?' Asked a teen with hair that resembled a heavily brutalized pineapple.

Young man had on a plain shirt and black vest, face caked in white like it had been rolled in espasol rice cake. Like other kids striving to be in fashion these days, this young man had on tight shorts and pointy shoes.

Who the heck was this kid? Delfin did not recognize him at all and had no time or inclination to find out. It didn't matter who this young buck was, really.

'Ah, I was visiting a relative,' he said, the practiced lie rolling off his tongue smoothly.

'Ah . . . Got that. Okay, you be safe out here and please give Butsok my regards.'

Delfin nodded and he quickly turned to walk away. Steps quicker now and hailed a cab at the corner. When he got in, he brought with him the fond memories of the district he'd shared with Edmon, memories that also carried with them sorrow and bitterness.

23

The first time he had met Buldan and Dodong was at a party where none of them had even been invited. They got in though, since they were buddies with the buddy of the birthday boy. Lucky for them that they got yanked by Onat into the party for Atong, who was the tribe master of the local Temple Street Gang.

Buldan, Dodong, and Onat were all out walking one night when they met Butsok coming the other way. Onat actually stopped Butsok and inveigled him to come with them to the birthday. Butsok that night was pretty clear in his refusal. He didn't know Atong or run with his rap-and-gangsta-loving, loose-pants crew. They weren't even on greeting terms.

Butsok was also worried about how the whole thing about him tagging along would look. Especially if he came in with Onat, known to be one of the most irritating fuckwads in their neck of Dreamland. Then he'd just be known as an extra hanger-on fuckwad, who came in with the guy already reputed to be the fuckwad elite. Same guy who'd already sleazed his way into a birthday he wasn't even invited to in the first damn place. Jesus, no way did Butsok want that level of drama.

'I'm telling ya it's all good and legit! Look, look, see Buldan and Dodong here, they're not invited either, my man,' Onat insisted.

'Got to pass on that, 'Nat,' Butsok held his hands up, looking at the two strangers named Buldan and Dodong. 'Maybe next time since I really need to just get home right now.'

'C'mon now, don't be like that. Hey, hey look, don't you know the items over there are free?' Buldan said with smarm, dangling the carrot, then sidled up to Butsok and hung his arm around him like they were just the bestest of buddies. 'How about we just go there for the item? Yeah, we'll just be acquiring items there, that's the mission, since everything else at that place of any use is that which we crave.'

Butsok relented and gave a shrug that communicated he might as well, but only really because he was getting dragged into it, and the second he stepped foot there would be the same moment he'd bolt homeward.

'Let's get on with it, I guess. Really can't stay long, ha?' Butsok said in the tone of a kid caught out past dark, worried about the already inevitable slipper-beating he'd get from his mother.

'Of course, of course,' Onat assured him. 'Once we're out of there, I'll even see you back to your doorstep.'

The three of them walked to the nearby zone, the adjacent neighbourhood. As they got nearer to Atong's house, they could hear the party before they even saw it. Huge speakers outside the house finally came into view, blasting Malabon Thugs' *'Momay'*—a song about the unbridled joy of smoking ganja. Above the noise, the party people hanging outside struggled to talk, the undeniable tone of teens and the young trying to outdo each other with their bluster and swag, argument, and brag, so that everyone would pay attention to them. Dodong and Buldan would furtively exchange glances, trying to confirm with each other if they really wanted the hassle of this silly scene just to score. Buldan seemed flustered by the noise and the inevitable need to engage with strangers. Onat was meantime eager to do any and all the vices available, starting with beer and marijuana.

'’Nat, you take the lead for us here, right?' Buldan wanted to confirm.

'No doubt, I told ya already right,' Onat said in an exasperated tone. 'Remember when we get inside Atong's, just relax while I finesse the shit. Eat something and get on a food trip. Then I'll get beers and items for us.'

'Chicks, too?' Dodong interjected.

'Fucking whoreson,' Onat shook his head and laughed as they continued to approach the house down the street with the ghetto speaker blasters. 'Nothing to worry about, plenty in there. Marry everyone if ya like.'

'I copy that haha.'

'’Tsok, you ok?' Buldan tapped Butsok on the shoulder and two seconds passed and he replied.

'Sure. I can't stay long, ah?'

The three just shrugged and scratched their heads at Butsok. When they finally got to the front of the house, Onat was greeted by his fraternity brothers with complex handshakes and a general tone that made it seem like they hadn't seen each other in a decade.

They small talked some more. Nothing but meaningless boasting, recounting what had happened at their last drinking session, who threw up the most, who got wasted the fastest, who drunk everyone under the table, who pussied out early and went home. The three stood there as Onat continued his exasperating social fandango.

'Oy attention please, this here are my friends from Dreamland,' Onat suddenly cut off the conversation with his tribe mates, starting to introduce the three.

''Nat, go buy some ice from Nympha's store. Atong's orders,' said one of the frat mates, ignoring the three standing in front of him.

'Ah . . . Well, okay then if that's what's needed,' Onat quickly replied. 'Where's Atong anyway?'

'Upstairs, with Gina. Doesn't want to be disturbed, you understand. Get going and buy ice.'

'Money?'

'Spot it, for now. He'll pay you back later. There's a bike over there, use that.'

Onat had no choice but to obey the master's order. Onat herded the three inside and gave them each a plate so they could eat while he bought ice. About to be left alone, the three friends found out just how full the house was, the party just starting to get on its groove. If the damn house had ears, it would definitely be complaining about the noise—made by human voices and the booming of the speakers. Same house would definitely judge the party-goers' idiotic shouting and striving to be heard above the noise while the decibels of the music were even louder.

'Oy, you guys know what to do? Food's over there,' Onat pointed to the dishes laid out on the dining table.

'Asshole, you better hurry back. Damn embarrassing, we don't know anybody in here!' Whispered Dodong to Onat as intensely as he could.

'Yeah, yeah. It'll be quick!'

Onat was gone and the three looked at their plates, trying to decide if they should stay put or actually make a go at eating.

Buldan shrugged and whispered, 'Dong, we might as well get something to eat. I'm starving.'

Dodong nodded but turned to Butsok. ''Tsok, what you say? Let's get some grub.'

They awkwardly tried to navigate the room towards the table, tip-toeing and dodging guests who always seemed to be in the way. Once they actually reached it though, people were still in the way. So they hurriedly just put any food within reach they could on their plates and went back to their chairs, off to one side of the living room. Buldan chowed down like a starving dog, swift in his chomping like he hadn't eaten anything that tasty in years. Butsok was way too nervous to eat, his paranoia acting up and making him feel like all eyes were on the three of them.

'Dong . . .'

'What is it, 'Tsok?'

'I think we need to get going,' he urged his friend.

'We just got here, what the hell. How about you actually start on your plate, eh?' Dodong pouted his lips, pointing to Butsok's plate atop his thighs where free and delicious food lay criminally untouched.

'Ey, I really got a bad feeling in this house.'

'Why.'

'They're all talking about us, is what it seems.'

Dodong looked around and said back to Butsok, 'Did you already do drugs before we got here?'

'No, no. I'm serious.'

'That's what I mean! Seriously, I mean it too. You were holding out on us and already scored,' Dodong insisted.

'Whatever, man.'

'Suspicions proven! Well, look here, why would they be talking about us at all, eh we don't even know anyone here?'

'It's what I'm saying exactly. They're talking about us because they don't know who the fuck we are.'

Buldan interrupted as he sighted the doorway, 'Onat's back.'

Just as Onat was putting the bike back outside a thin, long, and curly-haired man came down from the second floor. This was Atong. He intercepted Onat as he was coming in with two plastic bags full of ice. The three saw Atong whisper into Onat's ear and then glanced back at the three of them. Nodding, Onat hurried to the kitchen. Atong headed to the three friends. Before he could reach them though, people along the way greeted him and wished him well. The three stopped eating, sights nailed to the man coming towards their huddle.

'Hwuy, thass ess thwat Aytong,' Buldan whispered to Dodong, his mouth full and still trying to chew while talking.

'Fucking shit man, take it easy with that, there's rice all in my ear drum now. I know full well that's Atong,' Dodong replied, flicking away rice grains from his ear.

'Ay, so sorry bro. Let's greet him when he comes over.'

With a few more steps and a few more guests out of the way, Atong finally stood in front of the three. Buldan was the first to greet their host.

'Happy Birthday, sir!' He said, saluting weakly.

Atong only stared at them, feeling the three out, making them feel his scrutiny.

'These three, whose crew do they belong to?' Atong asked the room, his voice loud and almost above the deafening music.

The three friends looked at each other, glances that asked each other for help that was truly not forthcoming.

'Ah . . . we came here with Onat, who is our good buddy, sir,' said Dodong.

Atong motioned to a fat tween in the crowd who was squatting on the floor. 'Bodyik, call Onat over, he's in the kitchen.'

Bodyik went and Onat came running to them. 'These three with you?' Atong said sharply to Onat.

Onat hesitated, regarding Dodong, Butsok, and Buldan. Like he was trying to remember who these three were. Finally, Onat said, 'Don't know them, master. No idea who they are.'

Nobody spoke, certainly not the three friends. Like they all were frozen after Onat's declaration they were strangers. Their motherfucking alleged friend, who'd been up in their business for years and had all but forced them to go with him here, to Atong's party, had just denied knowing them. They all stared at the fuckhead with utter contempt and silent curses.

'Doesn't know you, is what he said. And I'm the one celebrating my birthday. I don't know you either and you consume my food like you're starving beggars,' Atong said, slowly and sharply.

His pronouncement was followed by guffaws from the drunk party-goers. The laughter sounded like crackling chicharon chicken skin in its sharpness, reddening their already humiliated and abashed faces.

'Eh, master, you think they might be fuckers from another tribe.'

'Hahahaha! Which tribe? The Yatap Motug Gangsta of hungry street bums?' Said someone in the crowd.

Another round of chilling laughter at their expense reverberated through the house.

'You useless shits best get the fuck out of my house now,' Atong flicked his hand, gesturing as if to flick away pests, like the three were mangy dogs that needed to be chased off.

At that moment the three did seem to accept that they were indeed hungry street bums, they were useless asswipes. What they could not and simply would not accept was how Onat had hassled them all. There weren't many things that could make them blush in shame but gatecrashing a birthday and the host kicking you out for trespassing and supposedly deceiving him that you were a friend of his friend was certainly at the top of the list.

The three stood and put down their plates. Without a word they made their way to the door. Miraculously, the crowd parted for them and let them do their walk of shame unmolested, albeit the stares and grins that followed them out of Atong's house as they tried to hurry without actually running, was enough to deepen the indignity of it all. When they were finally out of sight of Atong's house and the crowd outside, they breathed a sigh of relief and laughed at how absurd things had turned out.

'Son of a bitch, What I wouldn't give to see how our faces must have looked back there,' Buldan said laughing.

'Our plates were fucking smooth, man. We didn't even put them on the sink,' added Dodong.

'Ey, we got kicked out is how it is,' Butsok said.

'Oh 'Tsok, your face, man. Your face looked like you wanted to take a shit in the fucking saucepan!' Buldan chided Butsok.

'Ey, what about you? The man was already calling us starving bums and you still kept eating, eh,' retorted Butsok.

'How was I to know Onat was going to fuck us over? Plus, the chicken was just way too tasty, so I just needed to get all the meat off.'

'I wonder what Onat's problem was?' Butsok said.

'Like he was tripping at our expense,' Buldan surmised.

'If he did, he was probably forced to do it. Wouldn't think that way about Onat and being malicious,' shrugged Dodong.

'Forced to how?' Buldan asked.

'Well, you saw how Onat seemed like he's ranked even lower than a servant in their group? We just arrived and they already tasked him with buying the ice,' said Dodong. 'Nobody even glanced at us when Onat was saying our names.'

'Tsk. You got a point. I remember one time Onat told me how initiations in their group involved having to be in life threatening scenarios. Fool was boasting about the beatings, too. Said it took him a year of getting beaten down before he got in, so they'd be sure there weren't any weak members. Like an installment basis, see? Then I found out later from my cousin's girlfriend, who's also in their group, that he finished the required paddling in just two days. And here's Onat getting it stretched out to a year,' Buldan shook his head.

'Poor fuck. Had no idea we'd get involved in his stupidity!' Butsok said, still laughing.

Dodong cut them off. 'Let's go back.'

The two stopped in their tracks.

'And do what?' Buldan asked.

'Got a plan,' Dodong said, determined in his tone.

Butsok begged off, shaking his head, 'I really can't. I'll leave you to it.'

''Tsok we won't be long, I swear on my mother,' Dodong pinched him on the shoulder.

'But what are we going to do?' Buldan asked, still needing convincing.

'Don't worry man, we won't get hurt at all. When we get back there, I'll just get something,' Dodong said and turned to Butsok. 'Really 'Tsok I'm not joking, we're just gonna get something.'

The two relented and they all walked back to Atong's place. As they neared the house they took position in front of a nearby sari-sari store, about two houses away. Dodong was observing Atong's place closely.

Buldan asked, 'Dong, what now?'

'See those two bald fucks? When they go in, get their slippers. Or just get some slippers, any of them as long as you don't get a lot. Two, three pairs are good enough.'

'Fuck you, Dong. What for? You twelve years old? We're stealing slippers that look like they're halfway to being just rubber holes?' Buldan complained.

'Fuck this shit, you talk too much. Just do as I say. When those two skinheads go in, get their slippers and another pair!' Dodong ordered.

Buldan sighed and scratched his head. Then Dodong put his arm around Butsok. ''Tsok you see that black bike?' Butsok followed where his friend was pointing and nodded, sighting the indicated bike leaning beside the house. 'Get it when Buldan snatches the slippers.'

'Might be locked down?'

'It's not, I saw it earlier.'

'Sure about that, ha?'

'Definitely sure, cause that's the bike Onat used to buy ice.'

The three didn't have to wait long. There were times only Baldie One went in and Baldie Two would be left in front of Atong's house. Sometimes it was vice-versa, like they were guards. Then, Atong himself came out and seemingly sent both Baldies away on an errand. Atong went in and the Baldies left. When the two minions turned the corner, both Buldan and Butsok made a run for it. Like Dodong had ordered, Buldan scooped up a few pairs of flip-flops while Butsok made off with the bike. When they got back to the store Dodong already had two bottles of beers in mucho size and a gin. One in his right, the other under his armpit, and the gin already open in his left hand.

'Well, come on then,' Dodong said.

'Where to?' Buldan asked.

'You'll know when we get there. Let's make ourselves scarce before anyone notices.'

Dodong handed Buldan one of the mucho-sized beers, then they all piled on to the black bike. Dodong was standing at the back, feet on the extended back wheel joints, while Buldan rode seated on the frame in front. Butsok could barely pedal under the weight of his friends. They proceeded like this, awkwardly making a getaway from Atong's house.

Both still held their tongue despite wanting to know what Dodong had planned.

24

I could hear clearly how they were asking if I was awake, if I was conscious. Elmer's voice, I could identify easily. A tacit refusal to wake up was my overall strategy, despite all the kicks, punches, and swings they inflicted upon me to keep on waking me up. Who wouldn't want to just lie down and play dead? I ignored their rank piss sprinkling down on my face and chest but not the cold police truncheon that was being traced from my head to the crack of my ass.

The fuckers guffawed mockingly when I suddenly got up and crawled to a corner, folding myself against another anticipated beating. We're not at the station any more, I surmised. I could see Elmer and his three minions.

'You know what's hard? Trying to wake someone who's hell bent on pretending to sleep,' Elmer said to no one in particular. 'Worst of all is to make someone playing stupid finally fess up.'

Then he turned to me. 'Got bad news though, want to guess what it is?'

I kept quiet. He took a few steps towards me, squatted so that he could look me in the eye.

'The bad news, you'll want to know what it is I bet?'

Finally, I shook my head, more out of fear he'd turbo the thick truncheon into my ass if I didn't reply.

Elmer smiled, the smile of a hyena about to feed. I waited on his words that he consciously held in suspense. He'd turn his head and look back, as if trying to confirm with his two lickspittles.

'Now, now, don't worry, there's also good news. Which one d'ya want first, the good or the bad?' Elmer asked.

The feeling of wanting to number two tripled in my already fearful, rumbling belly. How good could this good news be?

'Up to ya, boss,' I said, respectfully.

'Alright then. I'm an easy guy to talk to. Let's go with . . . good.'

'Okay, sir,' I replied calmly, like my heart wasn't going to burst from the anxiety.

'Ah yeah, good news . . . We won't be killing you. The powers-that-be have tasked me with your safekeeping.'

I made an effort not to show emotion, just a blank reaction. Yet if it was up to me I'd prefer a quick death than this prolonged torment. Finish me off right now, *ora mismo.* Slowly, the reality that I'd be here for a bit as the brutalized pet of these sadistic fucks was sinking in.

'You don't seem happy?'

I didn't answer.

' . . . And now the bad news!' He said as he paced the room. I watched him walk around and the Elmer with the hyena grin now put on a serious expression, his brows coming down, his fists balled up, and the exhalations coming from him like an asthmatic village's worth.

'Bad news is the item that I owned, looks like you guys took a cut from it,' he said as he shook his head and flexed his arms.

Zero shred of an idea about what he was talking about. First, I had raped someone and killed them afterwards. Now I was the thief of some drug item. I should have died ten times over if I'd actually done any of these crimes, but the good news said that my current punishment would be an on-going project.

'Uh, boss . . . what item?' I asked with total innocence.

Now it was Elmer's turn to be quiet. His two goons advanced on me and grabbed both my arms, raising me to stand. I struggled. But they were too strong and with the weakness brought about by the many fucking beatings I had taken I could do nothing else but pathetically beg and struggle again.

'Boss, I-I know nothing about your item!'

'No?! Before your damn stingy friend kicked the bucket, why he even managed to mysteriously take a hit!'

Well, truth was I did have an item inside the biscuit can, along with Che's photo. That was what Buldan had smoked, I was sure of it. But again, zero idea what item of Elmer's I was supposed to have taken. Fucking pig cop wasn't making any sense.

'Boss, it was just something, some small thing we scored from around our hood! Believe me, boss!' I said in my defence.

'I know, I know. It wasn't much but it should have been the first and the last,' said Elmer blinking in fury.

Elmer picked up the police baton. I had a bad feeling about this.

'Boss, please no, what will you do?'

'Fuck your mother, my patience is wearing thin. I'd actually let pass what you did to Che, but the item? Where'd you stash it?'

'Boss, please believe me I don't know anything about your item!' I repeated my obviously useless mantra of denial.

Elmer walked behind me and pulled my already loose pants down. He ran the cold baton on the insides of my thighs, making my hairs stand on end.

'Again, where's the item?' He insisted. As I felt his rage emanate, I could actually feel like I wanted to be the person he wanted me to be, that I was indeed the man who had done everything he said when I was asleep.

'Please please, boss believe me. I don't know anything, nothing about the item.'

The swing of the baton was fast, and it came for the back of my head. I dodged it the best I could, yet I could only ever avoid a few of the repeated blows. As the hits became heavier, stronger, time seemed to crawl. Everything in slow-mo. Why were these thugs wasting so much of their time on me? Hot blood flowed down my face and nape.

Elmer mercifully stopped. Or he ran out of breath. My neck almost broke trying to look back at him. Even then I murmured my entreaties for mercy. My heart jumped again as I sensed he was gearing up for another baton blitz. I prepared as best I could. Keeping my balls to the front, putting my thighs together, and contracting my asshole to the smallest I could muster. Couldn't do anything about the shaking of my legs.

Elmer? He looked like a billiards champ who'd just gotten a great opening break and was now raring to get back to putting all the balls into their pockets.

'I DONE TOLD YOU I WASN'T GOING TO KILL YOU, DIDN'T I, MOTHERFUCKER?'

I closed my eyes. Tried not to breathe.

25

A second of peace is a true anomaly in a home where, for years on end, domestic violence was the daily rule of thumb. Butsok was therefore truly surprised with its miraculous appearance one night, like a dove descending on a war zone.

His father actually came home and greeted them without raising his voice, cursing them under his breath, or being in an all-around foul temper. His mother just stared at the old man, stunned. The miracle continued as Mang Delfin went straight to their room. No orders, no energy or gusto to raise his hand at his wife or child. Most of all, the damn miracle was that the old man wasn't looking for oil.

Butsok was already half-way to standing, aiming to get his father's hand for a *mano* obeisance when his mother caught his eye, signalling with her withering look for him to sit back down and stay the fuck put. So Butsok sat his ass down. He went back to sorting out his sister's pills.

Rosa meanwhile resisted the urge to offer her husband dinner or a cup of coffee. Distance was a good idea right now. There was great fear her husband would see her face and, realizing her bruises were healing, gain a sudden burst of energy to rearrange her features once more. Inside, she was rejoicing as both a homemaker and, most of all, a mother.

She had always been able to take her husband's maltreatment and would likely continue to do so until her passing. But for her children, especially Butsok, her soul died every time she saw them take a beating from this demon masquerading as her spouse.

Her son, especially, had lost his innocence way too early and had, as a consequence sought other truths, clinging on to them for dear life when he came of age. She had mourned the death of Butsok's childhood when she saw it happen and would take that horrible moment with her to her grave. All her fearful tomorrows ceased for a few precious moments that night, though. She wanted to savour every second it lasted.

Butsok had a different take on it. There's no such thing as incidental luck. There was only sorrow at the happiness of others. Always and likely for all his tomorrows. So, he knew that the peace his mother was likely feeling now was absolutely counterfeit.

Butsok stood and unpinned his jeans from the clothesline. Pulled them on.

'And where are you going?' Rosa asked her son.

'I'm off to buy Myla's meds. We need what's missing.'

'Son, you got money?'

'Yes po,' Butsok said, tapping the back pocket of his jeans.

Once outside, Butsok took a moment to reflect. He went to Lotlot's bread place and hung out there for a few minutes, people-watching and smoking a cigarette. Plenty of strangers walking, only one familiar face. The radio from inside the store blared out a love song. As advice for love sounded on the song's refrain he cast his thoughts back, way back to a memory that started at the curbside along Nakpil.

***

'How are you?' Greeted a young man Butsok did not know as he stood at a corner along Nakpil street in Malate.

'Pretty good,' Butsok replied, like he would to any stranger.

'Don't you want to go inside?' The man pointed to the bar.

'Um, okay,' Butsok shrugged as he studied the man's face.

'What do you mean "Um, okay"?' The stranger asked.

'Can't afford a drink,' Butsok answered.

The young man put his arm around him, and he didn't shrug it off, knowing exactly what it meant.

'With a good frame like yours, we can for sure work something out,' the man whispered slowly and close to his ear.

With that, he let himself be led, arm round his shoulder, to the bar and, once inside, was seated at a table for two.

Red light. Sexy jazz playing. All the tables were lost in their own little worlds, their own roads, their own styles of driving. The fiction above the table was different from the truth underneath. The stranger ordered two San Miguel light beers for them and a plate of peanuts. Butsok didn't even have the strength to muster any small talk. Trying his best to hide being new to the scene was pointless when he seemed surprised at everything around. Too much new stimuli.

'You're not used to this,' the stranger pointed out.

To which Butsok smiled weakly and took a swig of beer. Barely had strength for his mouth to work. 'Really your first time?' the stranger wanted to confirm.

Butsok shook his head. A 'no' with a smidge of nod in it. He wanted to mean both but was too embarrassed to say anything. He shook his head again, this time firmer in the motion.

'No need to be ashamed, it's okay to—'

'Well, I've been here a few times,' Butsok interrupted.

'Ah . . . Only seen you now, though, hmmm . . .'

'Might have just missed each other,' Butsok reasoned.

'You might be right,' the stranger shrugged. 'Some guys already tried to approach you before I did. You didn't go with them.'

'Didn't want to,' he quickly replied.

'But you did with me?'

'I don't think I can explain.'

The stranger just smiled and dropped it. Then he drank from the bottle like he was licking a lollipop, his tongue made circles around the tip. When he put it down, he winked at Butsok.

Butsok had no idea how to respond, so he avoided the stranger's hungry gaze. He glanced around, tried to look for the waiter knowing full well he didn't know what he'd order.

'You know, you look so very familiar,' said the young stranger.

'Oh, but you said it was your first time to see me here?'

'Just that you look like someone I know. You're way younger though, much more fresh than he is,' the stranger bit his lower lip.

To deflect, Butsok asked, 'You come here often?'

'Why do you ask?'

Butsok shrugged, 'Just asking.'

'Yeah. This is my job. Thought it was obvious?'

'Your work? Yet you're the one paying now.'

'When I say job, I don't always mean I'm the one doing the service. I also look for those who can give me my own due service. I am, as we say, looking to also be worked on like a professional works with pride on his job.'

More stories meant more beer. Bottles soon crowded their small table. People filed in. The scene was still alive even if it wasn't thriving. The young man asked for the bill. They exited the bar and called for a taxi.

The taxi weaved through the traffic, trying to get to the nearest hotel. On the radio, the voice suddenly sounded like it was a robot speaking. The driver fixed it by slapping the dashboard with his palm. The human DJ returned.

After a few weeks, Butsok's girlfriend Marife broke up with him. She was angry. She was disappointed. She hadn't caught him cheating, yet he'd still managed to give her a venereal disease.

That night with the young stranger had been the first and last time he'd been to Malate. Yet their sexual encounters had continued long after. The stranger had taken him to different places and Butsok had acquiesced to wherever he wanted. It was actually Butsok who'd insisted, though, on the different meeting venues. Owing that his girlfriend watched him like a hawk and he also had many friends in their neighbourhood. Even as far as Malate. The young stranger only ever nodded and took the lead in telling him where to go.

One Valentine's Day they'd agreed to meet at Lower Bicutan, with Butsok choosing the exact location in the area. They ate at a nearby Jollibee then left for their real activity's rendezvous.

Butsok brought him to Hagonoy, Taguig, promising a nice surprise once there that he said the guy would surely love. They finally alighted at a subdivision still under development, the construction of the houses a clear work in progress. The grass was taller than a man. No residents yet to bother them. They truly had the place to themselves for miles around.

The stranger shot him a sleazy look. 'My, but you really are naughty,' he told Butsok, pinching his thigh.

At a corner where the light of the lamp post did not hit, under the soft diffusion of the moon, Butsok's pulled down the young man's pants, removed his shirt. Fully naked now, Butsok told him to lie down.

With a flavoured lubricant, Butsok squeezed a good dollop on his hand and massaged it onto the man's already erect penis. He started jacking off the man, using his other hand to slap lightly at cheek and neck. Love taps. When he stopped, the man grabbed his hand and sucked his thumb in ecstasy. Sensing the other's heightened pleasure, Butsok bent down to fellate the rock hard cock. The menthol flavour of the lubricant filled his nose and mouth.

Butsok took away his other hand away from the man's mouth. He reached for his back pocket.

'Oh, you bitch, you motherfucker, don't stop don't stop, I'm almost there! Ohhh!' moaned the gay man under Butsok's ministrations.

Butsok felt fingers digging at his hair, pressure on his head as he was pulled deeper into the blowjob, farther in between the hairy thighs.

Butsok violently pulled his head free from the orgasming man. The sudden release made the other man gasp in surprise even as his cock continued to pulse.

'Fuck your fucking mother!' Butsok shouted as, with his other hand and in a swift, practiced motion, he slashed the gay man's throat.

'Ahhhhh! Urgkhgh!'

The man was too far gone to stop his ejaculation. His penis spurted out cum as his throat gushed blood. Death and an orgasm. The body under Butsok writhed like a fish out of the aquarium. Butsok continued to slash and stab wildly, repeatedly, like there was no tomorrow.

Each of Butsok's penetrative strokes was so intense in depth and pressure that the torso, legs, and arms were soon riddled with gaping wounds, holes that oozed out flesh and plasma like a pillow being removed of its stuffing. 'Ughm! Ughm! Whore son mugh!' When the ruin of all his stabs and slashes meant the body was unrecognizable, each hole almost overlapping the next, he pulled on the man's cock until it was stretched almost to breaking point like a rubber band and slowly, steadily, sliced, removing it from the balls. More blood was forthcoming. Like a firehose. Like a water gun aimed upward.

He then pried the jaw farther open and stuffed the man's cock inside then closed it. He found the man's briefs. Holding open the garter, Butsok put it over the ruined face like a vulgar death mask. He stood and spit at the devastated corpse over and over.

Deed complete, he walked away.

* * *

Standing, back at Lotlot's bread store, the shopkeeper fiddled with the radio until she found a news station. An update report on Task Force Pebrero was being recited by the DJ. Leads on the progress of the hunt for the Gay Serial Killer.

With half a grin, Butsok shook his head slowly. The police were corrupt without compare. The media were mercenary capitalists only looking out for their own gain. The people who believed either were truly like pea-brained birds, he thought.

26

I thought they were pissing on me again. It was a water gun. I had woken up to a kid, a young boy around five or six years old, shooting a water gun at me from outside my cell.

What a morning to get a rude awakening back in my cell. I turned away from the boy, the wetting from his gun making me realize how much my body ached. Most of all, my ass was definitely still pretty sore. Probably no use for rectal muscles if I did decide to take a shit. Couldn't feel my hips. Dried blood that had run down my inner thighs were still visible, tracing red rivulets and now coming alive again because of my sweat. My filthy cell floor was full of oily sweat. No doubt all from me, the sole occupant.

Trying to dodge or turn away from the kid's water gun was proving useless. Why even fucking bother? Can't even shoo away an irritating kid. Probably not a good idea to actually shout at him since he likely belonged to one of the officers. Apple didn't fall far from the tree, if that's the case. The young boy sure was having fun hassling me, knowing full well I'd get a beating if I did anything. No room on my body for any additional bruises, anyway.

'Vincent!'

The voice that called out came from near the front desk. Boy heard nothing and continued to shoot, dousing me with liquid from his water gun. Tried staring him down with my best *kontrabida* villain eyes. Little psychopath just went on shooting. An adult finally came into the room beyond my cell. It was Elmer.

'Dad!' The boy said, running to and hugging Elmer.

Makes sense now. This kid is Elmer's boy.

''Di ba, dada told you not to go in here?' Elmer lectured the kid.

'Yes dada.'

'He's a bad person,' the motherfucker pointed at me. 'You shouldn't be playing with him, okay?'

'No I'm not, dada. I am teaching him his lesson, dada,' the boy said, defending himself.

This motherfucking kid. Teaching me a lesson, is that it? Wonder what kind of twisted cop mindset Elmer's been brainwashing his kid's innocent brain with, saying he's not playing with me, the hassling from the water gun was just him doing his part for my eventual rehabilitation. The boy firmly believes that anyone on this side of the bars is evil. Well, he'll get his mind blown when he grows up and finds out not everyone who isn't in jail is a do-gooder.

Father and son went away.

I was fucking soaked. The boy had almost emptied everything from his water gun on me in his bid to teach me a lesson. Hell, the sudden quiet got me thinking again about what might happen later. Where they might take me. What else they'll pin on me. I wish action scenes in movies were true and it was as easy as that to escape from prison, fighting my way through dozens of bad guys with just my fists and wits.

The morning light was crawling towards me, so I did my best to slither to another corner, put my aching back to the wall, and remember all the shit that had brought me here. Events had happened way too fast for me to make sense of. *Was there another way out of this clusterfuck?*

Big stomping footsteps approached my cell. Here they come again. I haven't even stretched my legs yet and my heart goes pounding again. Imagine that? The fear still arrives despite how many beatings I take. The sweats and the heebiejeebies, they take over. Not to mention the rumbling in my stomach, likely directly connected to the repeated mauling of my asshole. Might not be able to hold it in.

When Elmer's thugs peeked in I made sure to ask to go to the bathroom. I also made sure to let loose a fart to welcome them back in style.

'Boss, please, boss. I really can't stop it,' I whined and begged. I was really, truly trying to clench my muscles and prevent the shit from erupting.

'Oy Cortez, that smell is nasty! He might crap in the van.'

'Just go, go. Escort the fucker to the toilet. Shiiit, I think I might puke. Smells like ghetto rat fart, for sure!'

One of them removed the padlock on my cell. The other motioned me out, not even daring to touch me. In their disgust I was able to hobble as fast as I could to the toilet on my own, clutching my stomach. How strange it was that all the faeces inside me yearning to burst forth had temporarily numbed the ache from the rest of my battered body. I locked the door and plunked myself on the throne.

Even before my butt cheeks hit porcelain, a wet gumbo had already exploded from my ass, some of it spilling on the lip of the toilet seat with its wide area of fetid effect. When the initial wet deluge passed, harder crap came through. Felt like literal shipping containers coming out my guts.

This was the direct result of the violence I had suffered from the night previous. After a few precious seconds of relief, all the pain in my body came back to my consciousness. I fought through it. Now was the chance to study my surroundings. Only a window set high as can be, with bars on it.

I shook my head and couldn't help but laugh at myself. Yeah, this was definitely no movie happening here. The embattled hero would simply escape through the window like always if we had a scriptwriter working on this story.

BLAG! BLAG! BLAG! Came the pounding on the door.

'Hoy, you fool! Finish up in there now!' Shouted the cop outside.

I saw a small pail inside a half-filled bucket on the floor. I dunked the pail into the bucket to wash myself of faecal grime. As I did so, I spied a container of muriatic acid to the right of me, near the corner. Got me thinking.

What was I supposed to feel here? Should darkness and anxiety embrace me now with such thoughts hovering right above? As I washed myself with the pail, dunking it into the bucket to be refilled over and over, I flashed back to Buldan, Che, and I, the prisoner of outlaw conscience. The whole miserable turn of events. And Elmer. That utter son of a bitch.

Even now I couldn't really fathom what he wanted from me. I kept on refilling the pail and washing my ass until the water in the bucket was almost gone. The line of thinking being formed behind my skull was like a tattered drapery being reassembled.

And now the bucket was empty. I opened the faucet. I maxed out the flow. Pulling up my shorts I stood and reached for the bottle of muriatic acid.

BLAG! BLAG! BLAG!

'Hurry the fuck up or I'll kick it open!'

. . . Acid. Likely now the only thing that arms me with a chance in hell.

27

To measure the stupidity of a police officer, it is said, you must not count the number of times the pig has fucked over others, nor how heavy his offenses are to the sacred duty of serving the everyday Juan. Instead, count the times he's actually protected law-abiding citizens. Tally those up and you'll be able to identify a total idiot of a cop who's clearly been waylaid from the revered path of sucking the giant cock of the government, the same body politic empowering him to be an instrument of assholery to his fellow countrymen.

In the case of Task Force Pebrero, we might then say that PO2 Castor was a veritable lightweight. As we got older, we also changed the values and truths we held dear, like, 'it is a sign of intelligence when one doubts and asks questions'.

The political circus that had formed their unit was truly no secret to its members. Yet everyone kept their cards close to their chest. Since they'd all been drawn from various law enforcement divisions, this made them instinctively mistrust each other.

It was just a job. All of it. Nobody took it personally. Not yet, anyway. All the good pigs had smartly kept quiet, avoiding drawing attention to themselves by keeping their heads down. They all valued their profession's privileges and perks. Asking questions was one of those pesky things that got you zeroed in on for unnecessary extra duty.

Nobody had made the mistake of asking questions. Not until PO2 Castor, at least.

In contrast to the known facts and conclusions of their investigation so far, Castor's own investigation showed clear anomalies in the interpretation of available data.

They, now, all sat at a round-table assessment for their task force. Castor had decided that now was the correct time to share his contrasting findings. So, he asked the presiding officer, SPO3 Malonzo, if he could speak up.

'Sir!' He raised his hand.

Everybody's heads swung PO2 Castor's way. First time anybody had raised a hand at these things but also the looks on the faces of his fellow unit members expressed as subtly as it could that he really shouldn't go through with it. They were worried for him. The worst case scenario was already playing out behind their law-enforcing eyeballs.

'Oy, Castor. Problem?' asked SPO3 Malonzo.

'Permission to discuss my findings, sir,' he replied.

SPO3 Malonzo's face wrinkled in curiosity and irritation. Everyone saw this reaction and the beat in his reply was conspicuous. 'Okay. Five minutes.'

'Thank you, sir!' PO2 Castor rose and, with a brown envelope, walked to the front of the assembly. He pulled out papers and handed it out to the group, having them pass it on to the officers next to them.

'The document you all now hold is a copy of my own separate investigation, my own findings on the gay serial killer we are tasked to hunt down,' he said as preamble.

SPO3 Malonzo raised his eyebrow as he read the paper in his hand. 'Get straight to it, Castor,' he waved his hand, his tone sharp.

'There are conflicts in the reports, sir. Thus, there is a problem in our public statements with how these killings are made by one person who is a serial killer.'

'So, you're saying that there's an irregularity with our prior investigation?' SPO3 Malonzo said.

'I'm sorry to say, sir. But, yes. Definitely.'

'Okay. Four minutes,' Malonzo's eyes were wide and challenging.

'Fundamentally, this means the killer's profile itself is an issue. The first victim was a thirty-five-year-old call boy. The second was twenty-two years old, a college student enrolled at a prominent and also quite expensive university in the U-Belt in Manila.'

'And so?' SPO3 Malonzo shrugged, impatient.

'Their profiles have a lot to say with the perpetrator's target and motive,' PO2 Castor swiftly replied, obviously prepared for such a line of questioning. 'The first case also reported that the killer took nothing, no items of value from the victim. Hence if this was not a robbery, we may typically attribute it to premeditation; an act of revenge.'

'Right. Actually. Revenge. In the case of the first investigation, we'd established that the serial killer had a deep-seated grudge against gay people. In his youth he might have been violated by a gay person. Through which was planted the seed of his future anger and blossomed into his current acts of revenge. Both victims were homosexuals, and they were both murdered the same way within a week of each other. Nothing more, nothing less,' explained SPO3 Malonzo as if it all should be blindingly obvious to anyone.

'And that doesn't justify that we have the same perpetrator, sir.'

'R-e-a-l-l-y?' Said SPO3 Malonzo.

'Second case,' explained PO2 Castor, 'Findings indicate that valuable items had been taken from the victim like an iPad, iPhone 5, a high-end pair of earphones, plus 25,000 pesos in cash that was meant for his tuition fees and confirmed by the parents of the slain. Yet, according to our reports, only one cell phone was missing and a 1,000 bill that was his per diem. To my point though, all of it aims at the bottom line—a robbery motive for the second case. No matter which way you cut it. I mean, it's pretty clear, sir.'

'And then?'

'Different targets and motives, sir—'

'What?'

'—doesn't make a serial killer and won't justify these two cases having the same perpetrator.'

'Both victims are homos, both were murdered the same way. Stabbed all over the body, amputated penis shoved into the mouth, briefs over their heads. What do you call that, Castor?'

'Plot,' PO2 replied.

'Wow . . .' SPO3 Malonzo chortled.

'Another important thing. In my investigation I found that the first victim and the suspect had a special kind of involvement.'

SPO3 Castor couldn't help it any more, he laughed. 'Wow. You must place yourself in the victim's shoes, Castor.

Think about it. You're brought to an isolated place, an empty lot with tall grass and you say you have a special relationship with your murderer? Who would go with an insane creep just to get killed at that kind of location?'

'Exactly. In contrast to the report, the victim was NOT forced to go to the empty lot in Hagonoy.'

'I can't understand you.'

'The victim would definitely not go willingly to such a secluded place if he didn't trust the killer.'

'And how would you prove the victim was not coerced and had gone with the killer under threat? Huh.'

'Sir.' PO2 Castor handed SPO3 Malonzo several pieces of paper. 'Lab results indicate that the semen found at the murder site was the victim's own.'

SPO3 Malonzo examined the documents like he was trying to ascertain if a bill was counterfeit.

'And I presume anyone would have problems ejaculating if they were sure they were at the brink of death at the hands of their killer. Pissing and shitting, maybe,' PO2 Castor added.

The rest of the unit was holding in their laughter. They couldn't believe it, but SPO3 Malonzo's face actually really did have the ability to get even more wrinkled.

'With that, we can definitely and reasonably speculate that the two had engaged in lascivious acts at the Hagonoy site. The perpetrator murdered the victim after he climaxed. The blood spatter analysis cross-referenced with the semen data bears this out as a high percentage scenario.'

The SPO3's mouth was narrow, the ends of his lips tight.

PO2 Castor wasn't finished, though. He pulled out photos from the envelope and held them up for all to see.

'This is very different to the modus in the second victim. See here, these are close-ups of the second victim's wounds. According to the medical findings . . . he was bound, beaten, then killed.'

The rest of the unit watched the scene unfold with rapt attention. Everyone was listening to Castor, and SPO3 Malonzo was keenly aware of it, adding fuel to his already simmering fury.

'We see now that both cases are very different. We cannot in good conscience base the motive of both killings only because the victims were gay men and appeared to be slain the same way. Truth be told, even if we're handed a dozen cases of murdered gays with decapitated penises stuffed down their throats and briefs over their heads, we can't pronounce those serial killings without clear evidence of the most important factors: *target, motive, and method of killing*.'

Malonzo sighed. He'd clearly had enough, judging by his red ears and blushing cheeks. 'You mean to say . . . there's no serial killer? That this task force should be immediately dissolved because it's a total joke?'

'Truth is, we have different perpetrators for these two entirely different cases. One's individually done while the other, is undoubtedly the work of a group. The second case is a copycat. Some group rode on the popularity of the first murder, the orientation of the victim, and how he was slain. Yet, if they'd done their homework there wouldn't be so many obvious blunders to their procedure. To me it seems like they really wanted to make it look like the first one, but were simply sloppy amateurs. So yeah, there's definitely no serial killer around. Just opportunists taking advantage of the issue,' PO2 Castor had gotten carried away with his passionate tone. He coughed and straightened his uniform, shrugged and said, 'Sir.'

'We're done, Castor. You've already exceeded five minutes. Don't worry, heads of the unit will consider your Sherlock Holmes-esque conclusions,' dismissed SPO3 Malonzo.

'Thank you, sir.'

PO2 Castor gathered the documents and stuffed them into the envelope. When he looked up, he saw the faces of his fellow task force members behind Malonzo beaming in pride, trying hard not to applaud. He drank in their silent praise and nodded.

Everyone kept their suspicions to themselves, though. It was an excellent presentation and excellent policework, yet, likely no good would come from it.

'And where'd you acquire your lab and medical reports, Castor? Did you get authorization from your unit?' SPO3 Malonzo asked as Castor walked past him.

'I have already exceeded five minutes, sir. Thank you.'

* * *

Three days later, the corpse of the brilliant PO2 Castor was found along a dark alley in Pasay City. Body punctured by dozens of stab wounds. Penis amputated and stuffed down his throat. A pair of bloody briefs masking his face. All were marks of the Gay Serial Killer.

The news spread like wildfire among the police force, fuelling gossip and speculation. Of course, many judged Castor, too, considering the serial killer only targeted gay men. Allegedly. These rumours eventually reached Castor's wife, six-months pregnant and in shock, unable to fathom or make sense of her husband's death. She'd never doubted her husband's sexual orientation. Until now.

Meanwhile, the members of Task Force Pebrero continued their operations unabated. They kept it pro forma about Castor's death, as SPO3 Malonzo and the other unit heads kept on revelling in the government's special funds—the monetary fuel that kept them alive, supposedly working to hunt down the still at-large killer.

28

Butsok had no other target for blame regarding what happened to his sibling. Only himself. In his mind, him ignoring twelve calls that day was equivalent to ignoring twelve pleas for help from his sibling. All for the fire that still burned in his soul since he was a child.

He was only nine when it first happened. Already waking up to the realities of the world yet still not conscious enough to be fully cognizant of the horror that would carry into and be the centre of his adult life.

It was the oil. The all-purpose lubricant for their father's gun that was always the first thing that ran out and the first thing that he wanted someone among them to go out and buy. That was all Butsok knew about it. Oil to clean his father's gun. Yet when he came home one afternoon, everything changed.

What changed his perspective was that afternoon, when his father drew him into the bedroom, past the curtain, then removed his shorts and briefs. His father spread the oil on his ass and inside his buttocks. *'Why, tatay?'* He repeated like a mantra as Butsok became terrified, of what, he didn't yet know. Until his father shoved him forward, positioned him forcefully to lean against the cabinet, so close into it that he could see the bedbugs at the back scurrying past the stack of his mother's clothes. That moment, when his father penetrated him, pumping his hips over and over, was also the same instant his perspective on being an obedient son transformed.

He was terrified to fight back. His father gripped his short hair like they were a filly's reins. The rending of his asshole was a pain he would never forget, the cruelty of it forever marking his memory.

Something warm fell down the inside of his thighs. His father's moaning was like the sound of a hungry beast. His motions were getting faster, more intense. Hips grinding stronger against Butsok's ass cheeks until he felt something spurt within him, a load he was familiar with yet never thought he would ever suffer. His father stiffened. And stopped. When his father withdrew a mix of blood, semen, and faeces came bursting out his now loose asshole. Butsok didn't even make a sound.

It was inevitable that one day his mother would catch them. And on that day, a humid afternoon, she pulled aside the curtain and saw what her husband was doing to his own son. The father didn't even stop, he blamed Butsok for everything. It came to a point where she was the one that was always directed to buy oil. His mother knew full well what this oil was for, that it would be used on their son. Not at all on the rusty gun. She would rebel sometimes and say yes, I will go out, yet never actually buy the oil. The jar was left empty. Yet the price for that was always a long night of beatings.

Many years later, nothing had changed. Only that Myla was now crossing into womanhood, a tween when she found out what was being done to her brother, yet everyone believed she didn't comprehend anything of the wrongness that it meant.

Butsok was well into his teens, by then. He would find himself sometimes, to his rage, sometimes waiting in the bedroom. Unable to remember walking in or even what had brought him in there in the first place.

When a body is conditioned over and over to an indignity visited upon it, it became normalized. Though he denied it to himself, Butsok realized he was physically craving the experience, that he now equated it as a sign of affection. He despised it. He had come to subconsciously like the violations. That by his father's acts he was the one who was favoured, the child given more love.

As he came of age, the rapes would become an out of body experience for Butsok. In Butsok's perception, he'd feel as though he was soaring and traversing to a different dimension whenever his father was in the mood for defilement. This was why, when he was being violated one night, he had not heard the twelve calls his sister had made to him on his phone. In the back of his mind there was a ringing somewhere. He thought it was simply because Myla wanted to be fetched.

Afterwards, Butsok waited for her to call again. It got dark and the call never came. Later that evening, his father took him again. It was the second time that day, and as he was being pummelled he began to worry about what might be happening to Myla. What could he do, though?

As his father realized his son's hole was drying up, here came the exhausted calls of the mother. She was calling for her husband. His father pulled out and put on his pants, and grabbed the nearly empty jar of oil.

His mother wanted to say something, yet his father came out aggressive, giving her a taste of his fist right away, and ordering her to buy oil as he pushed the jar onto her shaking hands. Butsok was still positioned against the cabinet, seeing his old friends, the bedbugs, when his father came back. His father mounted Butsok once more, as if they'd never been interrupted.

His father used his spit this time, wiping his palm against Butsok's nethers as they waited for his mother to come back with the lubricating oil.

IV

The Truths That Shackle Us All

29

The humidity could wither you on any given night at the Red Butterfly. This was one such night, the smoke clouding one's vision was from the escaping coolness of the asphalt. Twenty-something and teenage entertainers were in full force tonight.

While watching the other women cajole the horny dogs and street rats into paying for their service, she had time to meditate on something that had been weighing on her mind and will.

Red, violet, blue, green, silver. And darkness.

The colours changed, unceasing on her skin, and her thoughts drifted to how she might be even greater than a martyr, or a cat with nine lives. Elmer had already murdered her so many times. Killed her identity, her womanhood, her soul. Yet here she was, still surviving . . . only to die again when the sun rose. The club's blinking lights seemed to interrogate her overlapping palimpsest of bruises and welts.

She would decide enough was enough. Enough of this stupidity that had killed her for years, the fear that kept her under heel. She climbed to the dressing room. Put on her clothes and composed herself. She bid a silent farewell to the hell that, for a long time now, she'd tried to consider heaven. With her was a gym bag full of cold cash. All that money belonged to Elmer, and she knew this was a theft he would not ever forgive. A stash full of rotted dreams she once held precious, collected over a lifetime of suffering it seemed.

Goodbye to the Red Butterfly meant the beginning of a cleansing for her hopeful future.

The noise steadily died down until her heartbeat replaced the drum of the music and it was the only thing loud in her ears. She exited through the back, trying to evade every shaft of light. Walking swiftly, she murmured every prayer she knew under her breath. Petitioning the lord for a clean escape, that Elmer would not be able to trace her too quickly despite knowing full well he would eventually track her down and leash her again like a wayward pet.

It would not do for her ankle to be tied forever to a rock in the middle of a raging river. What she had lacked was the courage to leave. Until now.

She foresaw that the path she wanted to tread would be full of violent consequences. Nevertheless, she kept in her mind's eye two talismans: her love for her child, and her yearning for freedom.

Elmer had created the quicksand her life had become. It would be a true sin if she didn't even try to rise from its clutches. *I WILL be free*, she repeated in her skull and the speed of her steps tried to keep up with that wish.

Red, violet, blue, green, silver. And darkness.

These same streets bore her paranoia higher, because she had driven down these same streets with Elmer countless times. She felt his eyes on her even now. The intended harm in those eyes were heavy and threatening. This made her sometimes jog, sometimes walk. There was nobody there, every time she looked back. Yet, the fear remained. Her imagination fuelled someone's breath on her neck.

The club had now faded to a pinprick, its blinking lights yielding to the illumination of the moon on these avenues with dead streetlamps. Enough distance, she thought. She breathed, sighing in relief.

Then she gasped as someone, a man, vomited by the dark of the alleys, put his arm around her. Looking up she couldn't make out his features. He had on a black cap, faded blue jeans, and a white shirt. The pounding of her heart had resumed.

'Dong?' She queried.

Red was the blood that flowed from her chest as the man stabbed her with a rusty blade.

Violet were the marks that rose from her skin, when the man dragged her into the shadows of an alley, beating her with a two-by-two. Blue was the blood that pooled on her arms, legs, and chest.

Green was the grass that embraced her final remains.

Silver was the colour of the necklace grabbed from around her neck.

And darkness hid the grisly details of her wanton murder.

30

She'd been discarded like a dead animal at a trash landfill in Rosario, Pasig. Clothed only in bruises and abrasions. A woman picking recyclables from the hills of garbage spotted her, and was kind enough to bring her to the nearest hospital. When consciousness returned, she became aware of the ache in her injured legs. And when the doctor came in, he immediately informed her with a clinical, casual tone that she was now a cripple. She would never walk again. And then everything came flooding back.

Atsuo had been her devoted regular and it really felt like they had formed a good relationship. He was kind to her and seemed like he understood, even respected, the kind of service she had to give. Which meant he paid well. Sometimes he even tipped generously—never paying anything less.

Their last encounter hadn't seemed like it was anything but a regular night out. It turned out to be anything but, since, at the hotel room, after she'd bathed and freshened up for him, she came out in a towel to a fully naked Atsuo and his local driver, Renato.

They'd both been waiting. Her jaw dropped at the sight.

'Atsuo?' She threw the question at the Japanese man.

'Wwer jaz gana hab pan, my starrr!' Atsuo said, like a delighted child.

Then he turned around and grabbed Renato by his head, forcing it down and thrusting his cock into the driver's mouth. Renato received it eagerly. A shocked Myla had sense enough to back up to the bathroom, where her clothes hung on the back of the door. She left the two men and dressed. When she went back out, she was promptly punched on the stomach after opening the door. As she was doubled over, someone whacked her on the head. And into blackness.

She was naked once more when she opened her eyes. Lying on the bed, her hands above her tied to the bedframe's posts. Looking down, Renato was eating her out while Atsuo had mounted his driver, thrusting into him in true lust.

Her disgust raised the hairs on the back of her neck and manifested into a scream. 'You pigs, you sons of whores!' Myla shouted.

The men only responded in groans. Renato stepped back and Atsuo wiped his lips. The driver forced open her legs for his master, who mounted Myla with the same cock he had, moments ago, been eagerly fucking Renato's asshole with.

Myla could only writhe under the abuse. With what remained of her strength she begged, screamed, and cursed the two men who took turns raping her. The sheets eventually turned red.

Eventually unable to hold back, Renato and Atsuo positioned themselves on either side of her face, jacking off excitedly. Their cum bathed her face from the left and the right, stinging when the semen hit her eyes.

Finished, Renato rose from the bed and went to the cabinet, opened it. Atsuo had remanded to the couch and started smoking. Myla continued to weep.

'You sons of bitches,' Myla sobbed.

Atsuo went over and stood above her. 'Yu sharaaaap, *oishi*!' He said and slapped her playfully.

Renato came back holding a stainless steel baseball bat, to which Myla's eyes widened. He handed the bat to Atsuo, who caressed it.

'Say herro tu metal cock, Starr!'

'No, Atsuo! Please! Let me go! You fuckers!'

Atsuo traced the tip of the bat along Myla's legs until it reached her vagina. The cold of the bat cut through the aching tenderness of the rape she'd endured. Shock set in and she started to shake.

'Ahhhh! Atsuo, please!' Atsuo pressed the tip of the bat harder against her womanhood, adding to the ache of the rape.

'Yo rlirke tis, huh?' Queried Atsuo. And like reflex she spat at him, drenching his face in saliva.

'KUTABARE!' Screamed Atsuo as he angrily brought down the bat on her legs. Over and over again.

'AHH! AUGH! AHH! You fucking bastaaaaard!' she screamed.

Renato had had enough. He came over to literally put a dirty sock into Myla's mouth, gagging her. Thankfully, she passed out again.

Her family couldn't believe it when they finally got to her. The only thing they knew about it was that Myla, as she'd told them, was working as a helper at a beauty parlour. They were shocked when, during the course of the police investigation, the officers revealed she was a prostitute. Myla spoke to no one. In fact, the girl never said a word until they got out of the hospital.

Aling Rosa never faltered in following up her daughter's case with the police, hoping for justice no matter how elusive it would likely prove. They waited for days, weeks, and months without any progress on the case other than the name of the club where Myla had been employed.

Myla's brother, Butsok, had himself tried to make headway with the club. Yet no one would speak to him, not the other bar girls, nor the manager who washed his hands of the whole incident, saying their responsibility ended if the girl agreed to get 'taken out' by the customer off the club's premises.

Before he left one time, one of the girls had tried to press an envelope into Butsok's hands. It was a gift from some of the employees. They'd passed the hat and wanted to help with Myla's expenses. Butsok refused. He was not convinced that they knew nothing. He believed they were keeping something from him, something that could help identify Myla's perpetrators.

He'd made it a habit, after that, to go to the club as often as he could. With nothing to go on, he'd just stand across, or nearby, the place, observing the traffic and goings-on. Waiting for something to click. Anything to connect.

It was during one of these personal stakeouts that he noticed his friend, Dodong. The guy would also often be hanging out in front or somewhere nearby. Might be a regular customer? Butsok shrugged.

Still, he made sure that Dodong never saw him and continued to simply watch. Whenever Butsok would go to the club, he'd find that Dodong would also be there. He came to the conclusion that his friend was also waiting and watching. For what? Butsok had no idea. Had Dodong ever seen him? Maybe. If he had, he'd never given any indication he was aware of Butsok.

Through just loafing around and talking to people, Butsok would eventually find out that a woman called Cherry Blossom was someone managing the club. She was the one—and this was where Butsok's interest got piqued—allegedly in charge of all the traffic that involved the 'take-home' or 'take-out' of any girl by a customer rich enough to afford the exorbitant fees.

Rumour had it Cherry also got a bigger fee than the girl being rented out from the club. This very same woman, they said, was directly responsible for that girl who had famously been in the news, the one found naked and beaten in the dumping grounds at Rosario, Pasig.

Butsok wasted no time in finding out more about Miss Cherry Blossom. It was too easily revealed that she answered to the police. That the same band of pigs almost always fetched her from the club. Butsok had anticipated all this. The usual totem pole of criminal activity in the city was familiar to him. Yet there was one thing he was not able to foresee.

One night, as he walked around from usual spot to usual spot to observe the club, it was not the police but a familiar face who had come to fetch the pretty and poisonous Miss Blossom.

A familiar face with the same blood of a gutter rat of the Inners flowing in his veins—just like Butsok. It was Dodong.

31

Butsok immediately went over to Buldan's when he heard about what had happened to Dodong. His friend was about to leave when he arrived though.

'Brother, any news on Dodong?' Buldan greeted him.

'Ah, he got caught. Am just about to go visit him now.'

'It is what it is, I guess. Tell him hello for me.'

'Thought you'd like to come along.'

'Father wants me to go on an errand, so I only dropped by to get some news.'

'No real news yet really, not until I can get to him, ''Tsok.'

'You're back what time?'

'It's past 10 now,' he peeked at his cell phone. 'Likely I'll be busy until after midnight, ''Tsok.'

'Got it. I'll come back later and get updates.'

'Okay, okay. I got to go so I'll see you later.'

'Be safe out there, bro.'

They went their separate ways. Butsok climbed an incline road as he headed towards a convenience store near the entrance to the Inners and bought chips, loafed around for a while, and killed time. He monitored the hours and bought another pack of chips when he finished one. This time he stayed inside the store, taking advantage of the air-conditioning. When it got too cold for him, he went out to stretch and smoke.

A white van parked a few blocks near the entrance to Dreamland. He noticed two men exit the vehicle. Civilian clothes, yet with a different kind of bearing. He had a bad feeling about this. The two men strode confidently into the Inners without hesitation. Sweat beaded Butsok's palms. His whole body was clammy.

Butsok kept hidden and, after a few minutes, the two men came back. One of them was talking to someone on a big phone as they both entered the van. The van left, speeding away. He walked towards the loitering old men playing chess near where the van had been parked.

'They wanted to know where Dodong lived,' said one of the old men as he stopped playing chess to answer Butsok.

'And you told them?' Butsok shrugged.

'No choice. What if we took the heat?' Quipped the other old man across the chess board. 'Gotta learn how to spot the law when they come, son.'

Butsok could only sigh. He lit a smoke again and passed the time watching the old men play chess, walking around the nearby streets. A few hours later Buldan arrived, striding fast, clearly distracted.

Butsok intercepted him, 'Ey, how was he?'

'Dodong needs something done,' Buldan replied, his tone nervous.

Butsok put an arm around his friend, 'Police were here earlier.'

Buldan's eyes widened, and they both speculated about the worst that might happen as they marched to Dodong and Buldan's room. When they got there everything was a mess. Buldan immediately tried to assess the catastrophe of their things that the police had likely thrown around. Even in such a small room, the amount of worthless items they'd accumulated over the years was surprising now, when viewed through fresh eyes.

After a few minutes, he realized nothing had really been destroyed or tampered with, that they had really just been living like this as two druggie bachelors sharing a common space. He shrugged.

'You think the police really came here?' Buldan asked Butsok.

'Eh, that's what the old guys said.'

'Same old shit, same old mess. I remember where everything is, at least where we usually dump everything. Nothing's really out of place here, man.'

'Why'd the pigs ask about it, you think?'

'Never know with those fuckers,' Buldan scratched his head. 'Ah shit, I just remembered what Dodong wanted me to do.'

'Do what?'

'Where was it? Where? Where?' Buldan moved over to the cabinet and scattered the bugs ambling nearby.

Above it was a poster of sexy star Glydel Mercado, a hottie from the 1990s. Buldan removed Miss Glydel from the wall. Beneath it was a Zesto drink container made of cardboard, taped to the wood. Buldan also pulled it down. And behind that was a hole, about the size of an adult man's fist, where a small nest of what looked like hunchback cockroaches lived.

Their hiding place discovered, the vermin scattered, abandoning their roach hotel. 'Motherfucker,' Butsok said, surprised. 'The hell is that?'

'Dodong said there's some kind of can in there. A round one,' Buldan said and immediately thrust his hand into the hole. Focused on the task, he ignored the roaches crawling around his fingers and felt around inside. He came up with a biscuit can. He shook his arm free of the roach faeces and put it to his ear, shaking it.

'So, what's is it?' Butsok asked.

'Dodong said whatever's in here will be the only real evidence they might be able to use against him.'

Butsok and Buldan sat down on the mattress, their knees pulling up against each other on the floor in such a confined space. Prying it open, inside, the can had small amounts of shabu inside a sachet. The old meth balls were no bigger than peas. There was also some cash and photos underneath. Buldan held up each photo in turn. Most of it featured the same woman.

'Who's that?' Butsok pointed to the attractive girl.

'That girl who was killed. They're trying to pin the murder on Dodong.'

'Very pretty girl. That his girlfriend?'

'Yeah. Pretty,' Butsok nodded in agreement.

As Buldan continued to examine the photos, Butsok took advantage of his distraction. He reached over to his side. For what he was about to do, his heart skipped a beat. Angling himself away from Buldan a bit, he was aiming for some distance. Then he threw his whole weight against his small knife into a series of quick stabs. All of them hit with good effect, penetrating Buldan's neck like it was nothing.

'Tsowsskkrghk, wu wuh why?' Buldan had dropped the can, scattering the photos, and was trying to contain the blood spurting from his neck.

'Bro, I am so so sorry,' Butsok said.

As Buldan choked and tried to scoot away, Butsok stood up, trying hard not to slip on the blood. He followed up his attacks with more stabs, this time to Buldan's chest and stomach, making sure of their piercing impact as he stood over his friend.

Buldan fell over and writhed. Butsok, meanwhile, grabbed the other man's shorts and underwear, tugging it away until his friend's manhood was fully exposed. Then he pinched and pulled the withered dick, severing it with one clean stroke, a testament to the knife's sharpness and upkeep. The blood spatter was high and intense. Buldan's amputation had spurted plasma right up to the filthy, cobwebbed ceiling.

Butsok grabbed the small bottle of silver cleaner from his pocket and removed the cap from it. The rapidly fading Buldan had no strength to stop him. Butsok easily pried open his mouth and poured the contents in. He emptied all of it into Buldan.

Within seconds, Buldan's mouth had foamed and hurried along his demise. Butsok waited. When he was sure that Buldan was not breathing he filched a necklace from his back pocket. It was silver, with a heart pendant.

He placed it above Buldan's corpse, beside the bottle of silver cleaner. He examined the *mise en scène* he'd created. Satisfied, he quickly departed.

32

BLAG! BLAGAG! BLAGG!

The bathroom door was going to be destroyed and there was no answer from Dodong inside. The officers outside were feeling him out, knowing full well he had no way of escaping. The bars on the window were thick.

'Bastard. Come out here so I can slap you silly!' Shouted the officer that had escorted Dodong. He kicked the door again. Only silence from Dodong.

'Hey, what the fuck do we do?' He asked the other officer, lowering his voice.

'For sure, you destroy that and it's coming out your salary. You'll be dry for a month. Plus, you think about it, where are we going to shit?' Shrugged the other cop.

'Didn't say anything about fucking up the door, fool. All I'm asking is: What do we do?' Dodong's escort said in his defence.

'Keep on knocking. If the fuckface doesn't do anything we'll find a way to unscrew those locks, just don't break the door, fer Chrissake!'

The escort shrugged and, frustrated, scratched his head in irritation. 'Okay, fine.'

BLAG! BLAG! BLAG! BLAG!

'You son of a whore! You best come out now, or I'll . . . shoot you through the door!'

BLAG! BLAG!

'You're scaring the guy. He really isn't going to come out.'

'Fuuuuuck . . .'

More heavy knocks. Then, the door creaked open slowly, releasing a sweaty, stinky Dodong. His tummy was still turning from the looks of it, his head bowed in pain.

'Oy, here's the fucking bas—'

'Shhh, stop it,' said the other officer.

'Chief, I apologize. It's just that my tummy really was hurting,' Dodong said.

'Fine, fine. Elmer's coming back soon, go prep the van.'

'Okay, don't let this fucker out your sight.'

'You sit your ass down here,' said the other guy, pointing to the long, wooden bench.

The shouty cop went out to the van and Dodong sat on the narrow bench. He stood right back up when he felt something hard on his ass cheek. It was the water gun. The same one Elmer's kid had used to drench him. Dodong pushed it away and sat back down. The other officer shook his head and regarded him with pity.

'Ey, kid, if you still feel like taking a crap, you best go right ahead. Don't want an accident in the van now.'

'Would it be okay, chief?' Dodong asked.

'Just be quick about it. And answer when my partner knocks so we avoid the drama.'

'Oh, thank you po.'

'Fast now.'

As the officer looked away, Dodong easily swiped the water gun beside him. He was quick to go into the bathroom and shut the door. Minutes later, Elmer and his son arrived.

'Oy, Dodong in there?' Elemer asked.

'Yes boss, inside taking a shit. Diaz is prepping the van.'

'Oh, tell Diaz we're off soon and tell Dodong to shit faster. I still got to get my kid to his grandma's.'

'Okay, boss.'

'Pa, my water gun?'

'You left it where?'

'Don't know, pa!'

'Have you seen the kid's water gun?'

'Ahhh . . . No, boss. But I'll check if it's on the table. I'll be back.'

'Yeah, go.'

'Pa! Where's my water gun?' The kid piped up again.

'Just wait. We're looking for it.'

'Pa, my water gun, pa!'

'I said you need to be patient. You're starting with all that again, ha!'

'WAAAAAAH! MY WATER GUN!'

'Jesus, you wait here. Sit, sit. I'll go look for it, little pest!'

'I want my water gun pa! Pa!'

Irritated and exhausted, Elmer went to the other room and tried to scour the precinct for the damned water gun. He could hear his son still yelling and crying for it where he'd left him.

Dodong opened the door and whispered 'Pssst!' to the kid, calling his attention. He held up the water gun. 'Hoy, smegma breath, this what you're looking for?' He dangled the toy in the air.

'Gimmedat!' Shouted the kid.

Dodong held it out, cajoling, 'Here, just take it.'

The kid ran to him and made a grab for it. When the boy was near, Dodong tugged the kid and turned him around.

The child was now facing away from him. He put the water gun against the kid's head.

'PAAAAAA! PAAAAA!' Shouted the kid, asking for his dad to help.

Elmer quickly came back and, almost at the same time, the other two officers entered the room behind him. Dodong was now holding the child hostage and they all stopped to take in the absurd sight. The crying boy. Dodong with the water gun.

'Hoy, sonovabitch, you going to soak that kid's head?' Said Dodong's escort.

The three cops broke out laughing in unison.

'Yeah, fuck your mother too,' Dodong barked back. Then, to Elmer, 'You go fuck yourself and fuck your kid.'

'Soooo, you're going to give my son a shower? Moron!' Elmer said, then cackled.

'You laugh now. It'll be the last time.'

Elmer held up his middle finger to Dodong. 'Oooh, Dodong soooo scary. Just let him go now if you don't want a bullet in your skull.'

'I'll melt your boy's face before you can shoot me, idiot!'

The three cops looked at each other. Elmer visibly gulped. 'Dodong, you best let him go, sonovabitch,' said Elmer, fear creeping into his voice.

'PAAAAA! PAAPAAA!'

'We can talk, just let him go,' said Elmer's other flunky.

'We're all in the shit now. You can kill me but I'm serious about melting this kid's face, I don't give a fuck any more,' barked back Dodong. He tightened his grip on the boy's neck.

'PAPA! IT HURTS! PAPAAAA!'

'Dodong, tell me what you want. We can get an arrangement going, just be reasonable,' said Elmer, his tone now completely pleading.

'PAAA! PAPA!' Cried the kid, trying to vainly escape Dodong's embrace.

Elmer gestured to his two minions. 'Put down your guns.'

Elmer unholstered and put down his own gun on the floor. He stepped away. The other two cops were still undecided about it all.

'GODDAMN, PUT 'EM DOWN!' Dodong shouted and gestured as if to fire the water gun.

'Boss, he's just bluffing,' said one.

Elmer shook his head. 'Fuck, just lay down your steel.'

'Listen, boss. The water gun can't hold muriatic acid, it's impossible. It would melt the plastic!' Said the other.

A lightbulb seemed to go up behind Elmer's eyes. He stared daggers at Dodong, even with his hands up. He never broke eye contact as he slowly crouched, reaching for his gun.

'Just try it! Go on!' Dodong threatened. 'Aren't you all fucking idiots. This water gun is plastic, sure. And what's the bottle of the muriatic acid made out of, idiots? Steel?'.

Elmer stopped reaching for his gun. His face reminded Dodong of a woman who hadn't had her menses for six months, then was told by the doctor that, no, she wasn't pregnant at all. Elmer stood back up. Utterly confused.

Elmer sighed. 'Just put your guns down.'

'But . . . boss.'

'Fuck this. Do as I say.'

The two finally, reluctantly put their guns down and stepped away, like they were on standby mode. Elmer looked Dodong in the eye. 'Dong, please let him go. He's just a kid.'

Dodong stood and carried the screaming, crying boy with him. Taking a circuitous route around the tables and the three police officers. 'Don't make the mistake of following me, fuckers.'

'PAAAAA! PAAA! HUUUGHHHUH!'

'Where you taking my son, Dong?'

'I'll leave him a few blocks down. Again, stay inside and don't any of you fucking follow me. If I see your ugly faces peeking, I'll melt his ear off.'

'Dong, don't hurt him.'

'What now, boss?'

'Shut your mouth. I need to think.'

'PAAA! PA!'

'Get him at the second street down. I keep my word, unlike you lying bastards, you gutter rats!'

Dodong made a run for it, keeping one hand over the boy's mouth. He felt the kid weakening in his grip. After a few seconds the boy stopped struggling. When he got outside, he did his best to walk normally, yet walk quickly. He looked back. Nobody was following.

He still kept his head on a swivel as he walked down the street, one block down. Then the second. He put down the unconscious kid on a bench at a waiting shed. Dodong put a finger against the kid's neck. Pulse was strong. Probably just passed out from the fear and excitement. Assured that the kid was alive Dodong jogged away, and, by the fourth block, he mixed himself into the teeming crowd as best he could.

He wanted to cry for help, shout for aid to anyone that might help, yet his mind was weighed down by fear and suspicion. All he could see in his head was Elmer's face. Everyone wanted to make him suffer. Nobody wanted to kill him, true, yet nobody wanted to let him simply live, either. Where to turn?

When he was sure nobody was following him, he dodged into a dark alley. He sat down, right on the muddy asphalt curb and rested his back and head against a wall that reeked of piss. As he regarded the water gun in his hand he never noticed the tears rolling down both cheeks.

He burst out laughing, remembering Elmer's face when he thought the water gun really did have muriatic acid in it.

Dodong had almost been busted. The gun only had water inside, sure, but his quick thinking had rescued him from what would surely have been a bullet to the brain. Quick thinking and a good bit of acting. Only proved that Elmer and his filthy kind were morons without a brain cell to share between them.

33

It was no surprise to Butsok that Task Force Pebrero had copied his modus so they could profit off of it. It was almost comical. The second and third victims were both theirs. He knew this because the task force officers were great and constant customers at Menandro. In fact, he himself had embalmed their third victim. Servicing the police officer that had been a member of the task force himself, he saw first-hand how they'd tried to mimic his slaying ways.

According to the grape vine, Butsok had heard that the slain task force member had been ordered killed by the higher ups themselves. They'd done it because he'd figured out too much and was a pesky threat to their fragile money-making arrangements. And, of course, they'd killed him to shame him.

No problem. These events favoured Butsok's future activities, anyway, like they'd given him a lubricant for all his plans to pass easily into fruition. On the night of the victim's transfer to a lab in Quezon City, he executed one of these plans he'd been cultivating for some time.

The victims, you see, had all been stored at Menandro's preservation area—a storage room kept at arctic temperatures. SPO3 Malonzo had ordered all the bodies kept at one place so that, if they needed to modify or tweak anything in their condition, they'd have an easier time fixing things far from prying eyes.

Yet, after everything had been ironed out, the task force had nevertheless decided to transfer all the bodies to another laboratory. This was, they reasoned, for the additional documentation and examination that would reinforce the proof of a serial killer suspect. An angle that, of course, they'd completely made up.

Butsok prepped everything for the eventual execution of his plan. He put each corpse into its own body bag. Members of the task force even helped him load them into the transport, a mini truck filled with huge blocks of ice.

'Hey kid, tell your father we weren't able to wait for him,' said SPO3 Malonzo, then put a thick wad of 500-peso bills into Butsok's front pocket. 'Here's something for your trouble. Be sure to give him half.'

'Ay, thanks so much, chief! I'll be sure to tell Tatay. Thanks po!'

'Welcome. We'll go ahead, ha,' the cop waved a hand casually in farewell.

And with that, the mini truck departed, escorted by two mobile cruisers.

Butsok went back into the mortuary to clean up, his movements swift and precise. This way he'd have extra time.

He hurried home and, upon arriving, he immediately started packing his things.

'Son, what's going on?' His mother asked.

'Ma, quickly now! Help me, go pack Myla's clothes.'

'Why? Son, what is happening?'

'We're leaving!' Butsok said, his tone firm.

'But, where are we going, son?'

'Jesus! If you want to stay and die in this hellhole, I'll leave you to it. But I'm taking Myla! Fuck this shit!'

'I'm coming with you, son, but your father. He'll find us! He'll kill us!'

'Ma, he'll never be able to hurt you again. Believe me! Now, pack up and be quick! We don't have much time.'

'How will we live, son?' His mother kept on bugging him even as she did as told and started packing.

'I've got enough saved up. Just enough for us, just enough for a new start.'

The nerves had gotten the better of his mother and whatever she grabbed, hangers and clothes, all seemed to fall off her butter fingers. Butsok went to get his sister. He slung her scrawny form on one shoulder. Eventually they were set and, not wasting a look back, exited their house, heading to the taxi stand near the entrance to Dreamland. Luckily, Butsok was able to flag one down right away. He loaded their bags into the trunk, with the help of his mom they put Myla in the back as gingerly as they could, and then they all got in.

'Where to, boss? The driver asked Butsok, who was in the passenger seat.

'Boss, take us to Baclaran. The bus terminal.'

* * *

The task force convoy arrived at the laboratory and, right away, the bodies were brought into the chilly morgue, lined up like cured hams. SPO3 Malonzo and crew were taken by surprise though, when two police officers, helpers who were not from their unit, unloaded an extra body bag.

'Boss, this one was under one of the others. Feels heavy,' explained the officer.

'Uh, wait. What in hell? Ey, there's only three corpses that's recorded on our hands.'

'Might have been an accident, maybe it just got mixed in, boss,' interjected one.

'Yeah, just put that in with the rest. Be sure to count them,' SPO3 Malonzo said, trying to regain his composure.

Two of the lab personnel opened the body bags and, when they reached the last one, the extra one, out spilled three decapitated heads and various other chopped body parts. The lab techs saved them from falling and took them out, lined them up too like grisly table decor. The task force officers knew one of these heads, but the other two were completely unfamiliar.

'Sonovabitch!'

'Fuck, chief, isn't this the head of that mortician at Menandro?'

'The kid!'

'Fucking hell! SHIT!'

Chaos erupted among the task force officers. They simply could not believe it, yet they knew at once what had happened. That young mortician at Menandro had actually had the balls to do something, something they thought only police like them possessed the boldness for.

The lab door slowly opened. More panic set in when the task force cops saw another completely different set of officers from a different unit come into the room.

'Good evening! I am PO3 Alvarez po, chief!' The leader of the visiting corps said, saluting SPO3 Malonzo.

'Good evening as well. Something I can help you with, brother?' Said SPO3 Malonzo, regaining his professional calm.

'Ah, wanted to talk to you, sir,' he replied.

'If you want to use the lab, kindly wait until we're finished.'

'Not exactly.'

'Well, if you're not going to use the facilities are you saying you have an operation here? In the area?'

'To be clear, chief, we have no operation. And no, we do not intend to use the lab.'

'So, what can we do for your team?'

'We're here to observe.'

'Observe what?' SPO3 Malonzo's tone was sharp.

'The examinations,' said Alvarez from the new unit.

'Look, this is a very serious ca—'

'We're here not to intrude, chief,' Alavarez interjected, cutting off SPO3 Malonzo.

'We're here because we're ordered to be here and observe. That's it.'

There were six members in Task Force Pebrero, including SPO3 Malonzo. In contrast, the other unit had nine officers. With the tension rising, each side couldn't help but size up each other. If there was going to be a fight, everyone cast their thoughts on who to fight and how, girding loins and constricting asses into readiness.

'Where's your order?'

PO3 Alavarez pulled out a piece of paper, folded like a Meralco electricity bill, and handed it over to SPO3 Malonzo, who read the thing.

He shook his head and sighed. 'Okay, then . . .' relented SPO3 Malonzo.

Nerves eased, the lab personnel proceeded to remove the corpses from their body bags. PO3 Alvarez and his team indeed kept silent and observed, while SPO3 Malonzo and his crew could only anxiously watch the lab staff and the other unit.

PO3 Alvarez noticed the last bag, 'What about that one? Why hasn't that been opened all the way?'

'Bro, those contain all the chop-chop body parts. Obviously, we put them all in one bag so the meat wouldn't spill out and the evidence damaged,' SPO3 Malonzo's voice was dripping with sarcasm.

PO3 Alvarez merely nodded in acknowledgement and continued to watch. The lab people laid out their tools onto a long tray, they arranged small bottles and huge syringes.

One lab tech wrote on a notebook as he pinched and poked at the corpses, feeling their arms, stomachs, and cheeks. Another started injecting something into the bodies. The police could simply watch and wonder at these doctors of death, unable to comprehend the procedure with their impoverished minds.

Slowly, SPO3 Malonzo started to relax. And seeing that he had relaxed, his crew's anxiety eased, too. Until one of PO3 Alavarez's crew stepped in and started to poke and pinch one of the bodies.

Surprised, one of Task Force Pebrero's members piped up. 'Wait . . . wait! Bro, can you tell your officer that your orders are only to observe. Right?'

'Better read the paper again, chief. 'Cause what he's doing is part of the observation.'

'Mario, let them,' SPO3 Malonzo shook his head, telling off his own officer.

'Sorry, sir.'

Later on though, the same officer from PO3 Alvarez's team picked up a scalpel. Then he'd thrust it into the stomach of one of the bodies.

'What the hell are you doing?!' SPO3 Malonzo said.

The cop had reached into the wound he'd made and put his hand inside. He was feeling for something inside.

'And what the fucking hell is this, chief?' The cop had pulled out a big, translucent plastic bag that had white crystals inside.

'Wu-wa-what's that?' Said SPO3 Malonzo, his lips trembling, barely able to articulate his rage.

'We don't know, chief,' shrugged PO3 Alvarez. 'Go ahead and cut those open,' he added, waving to his team.

Now the whole unit under Alvarez stepped in, picking up scalpels of their own and slicing open the stomachs of every one of the still intact corpses. Each one had its own plastic bag of white crystals. Like blue balled cocks, the Task Force Pebrero cops could only watch as their evidence was unearthed, while SPO3 Malonzo felt like he was drowning in quicksand that had come out of nowhere. This was not part of any racket they were involved with or had been profiting from.

'Let me reintroduce myself, chief. I am PO3 Alvarez, from the Metro Manila Anti-Drug Task Force,' said Alvarez. 'Everyone calmly come with us and there'll be no trouble.'

'Trouble? What the fuck is this? Sonovabich, we're all police here, we're all pigs, you fools!'

Alvarez grinned. 'Not all of us. Or maybe just some of us, some of the time.' To which the rest of the anti-drug police laughed. 'See, we got a tip that you fine officers were using corpses as shabu couriers, chief. It is what it is. Nothing personal. Our job is simply to carry out our orders. Maybe you know, you pissed off some big businessman up top. Who knows these days?'

SPO3 Malonzo was speechless as cops from both sides looked like they were about to brawl. Some officers from Task Force Pebrero were refusing to be cuffed. Tensions in the lab inevitably ratcheted up.

Outside the lab building, passersby heard consecutive shots fired, one after the other.

* * *

Inside the taxi, Butsok laid his forehead on the car door's glass. He watched the people outside, walking under the midnight sky. He was hypnotized by the lights on the posts sparkling as they passed, the neon signs and the headlights of the vehicles going the other way.

Checking on his mother and sister in the rearview every few minutes, he sighed and shut his eyes. As he recalled what he'd done and relived the choices he'd made, the tears flowed down his cheeks.

Quickly, he wiped them off with the back of his hand. Again, he shut his lids. This time he slept.

34

The barangay marshals woke up the whole neighbourhood that morning. Dodong and Buldan were still rubbing away crust from their eyes when, peeking out the window to investigate the racket, they saw the marshals dragging away their friend Onat.

Onat might be a bastard, but they still felt bad for him. Buldan went out to get any gossip from the gathered crowd.

'Why'd they pick up Onat?' He asked a woman with a child in each arm.

'Eh, they said that group had burned a house down over at the other end. All of them likely drunk, probably was just another trip for them, you know.'

'Ahhhh . . . Other guys also got caught?'

'Said they're already outside, got them piled in like sardines in the barangay van,' said the woman, pouting towards the direction of Dreamland's exit.

Buldan wasted no time walking back home and telling Dodong everything he'd heard.

'They took in Onat, and they already got the others at the barangay van too.'

Dodong said laughing, 'Got what was coming, the fucking bastards!'

'Fuck, Dodong, you're a genius!'

'But of course. It's just Butsok and you who had no faith, eh!'

'I was a believer from the start!' Buldan said, holding up his hands. 'Butsok has to hear this, let's share the good news!'

'Good idea, let me throw on something.'

Both of them got dressed to go out. Before they headed over to Butsok's place they went to where the marshals had taken the suspects, inside the barangay's vehicle for boisterous drunks and petty criminals. The vehicle, the Ampra, was an old van, more specifically an ancient model that had definitely seen better days, fitted with modified vertical rails akin to prison bars welded to its windows. The friends were eager to see what had happened.

Atong was there. So different in demeanour from the Atong who had shamed them at his house. Like a puppy scared of people, about to piss himself. Behind the Ampra's bars Atong seemed way too nervous to even stroke the steel on the van's window or lay down on the cold and filthy floor. Hard to believe this was the same guy who'd confidently shamed them and kicked them out at his birthday party. The same one who had zero hesitation to bully the weak and to strike those he knew would not strike back.

Buldan and Dodong approached, the bars of the Ampra were the only barrier between them and Atong's gang.

'How we all doing in there?' Buldan said cheerily.

Atong stared back daggers but Onat said nothing. Some among them were even sniffling as quietly as they could.

'Pro tip. Next time you try and burn down a house, try not to leave your slippers and bicycle outside.'

Atong got over his shock after a beat and tried one last shot at bravado. 'You two fuckers are dead when we get out of here!'

'Get out? Ay, I don't know about that, friend. I hear there was a senior citizen who unfortunately died in that house you guys torched. Chances of getting out are likely slim. And, well, I say fuck you all,' Buldan said.

'You sons of whores!' One of Atong's gang members piped up behind him.

BONG!

The *tanod's* acacia stick struck the van's bars and made a dull ringing as it percussively hit each one. His red eyes betrayed either drunkenness or insomnia. The two friends said goodbye to the suspects with their smiles and middle fingers on display. They laughed as if it was all pure comedy.

Dodong put his arm across Buldan's shoulders and whispered. 'Bro, are you sure that we killed a senior when we did it?'

'Ay, you idiot, I was kidding. Just wanted to see the fear in those fuckers' eyes.'

'Put it there!' Dodong put a palm up.

The friends high fived, their palms hitting each other with a sharp crackle. They walked on past the commotion, heading for Butsok's place. They bravely shouldered into the crowd, not caring who they bumped into, who they tripped or hassled. Let the bastards whine and whimper.

Walking on, they were determined to tell their friend the great news.

Acknowledgements

I don't think I'd have lasted a decade in writing if it wasn't for those who believed in my storytelling, that it was, even for a bit, consequential. Yet for as long as I'd been doing this I have yet to experience a formal writing workshop, so whenever I'd finish a story the first people I'd dare to disturb were friends and family. As my primary workshop panel, they'd be the first to say if my stuff sucked. But if they declared I'd somehow written a winner, my confidence would get a boost and only then would I feel I could let others read it.

Many thanks to the good friends who've never once faltered in listening to or reading my stories. From the beginning up to now, these have been the comrades who've greatly inspired me. Know that your support has always strengthened my spirit: Ronnel Vivo, Angelo Arispe, Erwin Dayrit, Danell Arquero, Earl Kristian Palma, Christian and Michelle De Jesus, Jason Cruz, Raffie and Karol Lacuesta, Leslie and Iane Cotas, Benjamyn and Joan Tanyag, Robertson Darang and Sheryl Roldan, Lee Anjelo and Glady Gutierrez, Praisel Arlo Cruz, Liora Kennevee Santillan, Patrick John Vivo, Jinky Catalan, Regie Capco, Jaren Nabaonag, Kai Osorio, Mark Anthony Villegas, and Kristan Joerick Dasco.

To Karl De Mesa, for crafting the bridge into English this novel was able to march on, and thus the opportunity to be read in different corners of the world.

My fellow creative brethren: Jay Jumawan, Markus Bulandus, Joy at Karis Legason, Jon Beaquin, Adam Carlo Along, Erik Tuban, Bobby Legaspi, Rallye Ibanez, Gani Simpliciano, Arturo 'Fletch' Del Prado, James Lorrence Ocampo, Ben Baladad. To Nico Garduce, Dwight Galang, and the rest of ARPAK. To Angelo Suarez, Ma'am Nida Ramirez, Rick Olivares, Bogs, and Italo.

To Dean Ederson Tapia, Prof. Pompeyo Adamos III, Prof. Linber Allan Eugeinio, Prof. Jepthe Munez, my professors at CCAPS, University of Makati.

To Maria Rosela Ricamara, Micah Gaylican, Sarah Jane Bataller, Imee Jean Sanchez, Guadalyne Suarez, Julie Rebucas, Joey Bucayu, Liesian Tamunday, Erick Neri, Kevin Guinto, Apple Bacusa, Arny Realosa, Gem Amboy, Jaime Tallada, Roel Barbosa, Pamela Orlanda, Julie Cruz, Jasper Aquino, Chek at Cromz Alcantara, Jefferson Lago, Fatima Decena, Jelly Rose Aragon, Otits Patrick Reyes, Janna Mae Ojales, Khristine Mae Delafuente, Rowena Zaballa, Ann Escalante, Lisa Macatangay, Evalyn Evangelista, Nona Miranda, Annie Salazar, Jamie Roque, Boyet and Elsa Tan, Darcy Aniasco, Ivan Ala, Jayden Manumbale, Jesus Israel, Murkz De Vera, Vincent Parafina, Alex at Cecil Alfonso, Len Antido, Limuel Maquilan, Jennifer Macas-Napao, Boss Merlina Panganiban, and Sir June Bawisan.

To the Famador family: Judith, Panfilo, Ron, Claire, Edward, Era, Alab, at Francis.

For Olivia Himig Vivo and Juambai Famador.

To the Soledad and Vivo family, my cousins, uncles, and aunts who tell such delicious stories of their own experiences. Many times, it is from them that my own stories are cribbed from as homage. Tito Junior, Insan Jhayl, Athan, and Marie. To the family, Ate Jho, Karen at Dada, Mga Pamangkin, Joshua, Justine, Agatha, Jaja, JE, Natahlie, Jared, Jacob, Khole, Jayden, Kyrus, Nhil, Alonzo, Isabelle, Gab, and Tito Weweng.

For Tita Cristy Neuman, Tita Soledad Murray, Ronaldo at Lagrimas Vivo, Ronilyn and James De Guzman. I hope this token of gratitude may act as small recompense to your generosity, however modest.

And to all the readers who've never wavered in their support for this kind of literature, I sincerely hope to one day be able to simply hang out with you all.